"MY D⸎   ⸎nd and smoothed
d⸎

                                ⸎ that's just because
the⸎   ⸎d us to stay under-
gro⸎   and show the world
wha⸎   ⸎ are⸎   ⸎e are in control—
and w⸎ ⸎⸎he⸎ ⸎ontrol, ⸎⸎ ⸎⸎o mistake about that—the
p⸎   will⸎   ⸎xactly wh⸎⸎ they stand. The
                ⸎nd the ⸎⸎⸎k will fall by the wayside.
              ⸎⸎ored. It's ber⸎⸎ ⸎ everyone, and once
          ⸎ realizes that, they'll⸎ ⸎icome u⸎ with open arms.
⸎⸎⸎⸎ me."

              ⸎⸎⸎⸎
                  ⸎⸎ade said.

                ⸎," Alex replied automatically.

              ⸎ out of the War Room, Alex's mind flickered
wit⸎   ⸎   the day.

              ⸎future he⸎⸎ ⸎⸎ promised himself one
thing: H⸎   ⸎⸎ ⸎   ⸎en Cloak defeated
the R⸎ ⸎

JERAMEY KRAATZ

HARPER

An Imprint of HarperCollins Publishers

Library of Congress Cataloging-in-Publication Data
Kraatz, Jeramey.
    The cloak society / Jeramey Kraatz. — 1st ed.
        p.   cm.
    Summary: Alex Knight, a twelve-year-old in training to be a
supervillain in the elite Cloak Society, becomes friends with a young
superhero and begins to question where his loyalty lies.
    ISBN 978-0-06-209548-0 (pbk.)
    [1. Supervillains—Fiction.   2. Superheroes—Fiction.   3. Mothers
and sons—Fiction.   4. Loyalty—Fiction.]   I. Title.
PZ7.K8572Clo 2012   2011044635
[Fic]—dc23
Typography by Torborg Davern
13 14 15 16 17   OPM   10 9 8 7 6 5 4 3 2 1
❖
First paperback edition, 2013

For Mom, who taught me the importance
of being myself.

CONTENTS

THE CLOAK SOCIETY

A BIRTHDAY
HEIST

You don't just fall into supervillainy. It's not like theater or baseball or the after-school club you join because all your friends are members. Supervillainy is a way of life. It's something you must want with every fiber of your being. You have to wake up every morning thinking, "Hey, this world is mine for the taking," and mean it. Most people don't comprehend the passion needed to be successful in such a thankless field, one that boasts such a low rate of success. It's not all doomsday devices and dramatic entrances. Your days are spent plotting, strategizing, inventing, training—trying to prove to your city or your nemesis or yourself that you're not just some delusional screwup who read one too many comic books. Every day you face humiliation, rejection, and failure. It's a life that requires bravery. If you call yourself Captain Terror or Madam Fear, you'd better be able to live up to the name. When you're backed into a corner, you can't hesitate to use your death ray.

Supervillainy also takes patience. You have to lie in wait, lurking beneath the surface and watching for the perfect time to strike. Countless would-be criminals have met their demise because they threw on a domino mask and headed to the nearest bank without proper forethought. You see it on the news all the time. Just last month a man in Chicago accidentally turned himself into a human Popsicle during what should have been a routine jewelry heist, because he failed to properly test his homemade freeze beam. It took two days of defrosting before police were able to fingerprint him. A week later, in Phoenix, a man decked out head-to-toe in black leather passed out from heat exhaustion while running from authorities, completely unprepared for physical exertion in such an unforgiving material. And that same day, a caped woman managed to infiltrate the Los Angeles mayor's home and abduct his five-year-old son. Unfortunately, her escape route led into a linen closet. By the time she found her way out of the mansion, she walked straight into the arms of a SWAT team. Had she visited the local library to research the house's floor plan, she might be lying on a beach somewhere counting her ransom money instead of sitting in a dank maximum-security cell. In a way, such incompetence is a blessing for the *real* villains. It lulls the world into a false sense of security.

"Supervillain" is a title that's earned from the fearful public, not one that's self-ascribed. The good ones have already won by the time their identities are revealed. The best are those you've never heard of.

Of course, some of the most successful supervillains are those who were born into the life. You could decide today to devote your existence to some nefarious plot and spend the rest of your years training exhaustively, but your skills would never be on a par with those of someone who was learning to escape from handcuffs at the age of four. These kids are brought up to value domination and conquest, fueled by a sense of superiority. It is this small group—reared to devote themselves completely to the aims of their parents or guardians—who grow to be truly feared, for they believe their actions to be unquestionably right. That the world really would be a better place were they in charge.

Supervillainy is not for everyone. It can be a lonesome life. Victories, for the most part, are personal. Heroes are the ones who get the glory. For them, it's all press conferences and guest appearances on talk shows and monuments dedicated to their achievements. And they work so well together in teams, parading around the city in their matching capes and uniforms. For them it's easy. A hero's goal is well defined—stop the bad guys, save the city, maintain the status quo. It's not so simple for a team of people who romanticize revenge and thievery. In the end, the individual members of supervillain teams are usually just looking out for themselves. Their camaraderie is a sham, and this almost always leads to defeat.

One team is an exception. Its founders were scientists tasked with researching new forms of weaponry during the Second World War. When their experimentation became unorthodox and dangerous, the world turned on them. The scientific community called them mad. The government threatened to imprison them if they continued their work, so the scientists took their research underground. There, they uncovered a powerful energy that existed outside the known electromagnetic spectrum, a radiation like science had never before seen. They called it Umbra. The scientists tried to harness it, but it was too powerful, too volatile for domestication. They were dismayed, but soon learned that their work had not been without benefits. Their exposure to Umbra had unique side effects: The team of scientists had developed uncanny abilities. They were now something more than human.

When the government officials and the scientific community heard tales of these developments, they were all quick to heap praise on the rogue scientists they had once spurned. After all, this scientific breakthrough could be the first step in a new age of human prosperity. But by this time, the scientists had grown as bitter as they were power-ful. They destroyed all their research and vowed revenge on the world that had turned its back on them. They promised to one day rule over the weak-minded. It was this common bond and feeling of having been betrayed that helped form the most successful supervillain alliance in history. They were a team first, criminals second. They called themselves the Cloak Society.

Sterling City, Texas, gleamed in the blistering mid-September sun. The sprawling metropolis had been called the birthplace of the twenty-first century, a trophy of humankind's progress and achievements. Its reputation as a thriving city rivaled that of New York and London and Tokyo. People all over the world flocked to it, and con-struction never seemed to cease as it expanded in every direction like a growing puddle of business and industry. It was a place of cement and steel and limestone and glass, of video billboards and corporate headquarters. Victory Park was at the center of it all, over five hundred acres of well-manicured lawns and tall trees and monuments all contained in a perfect circle. Ringed around the park were the arts district to the north—cavernous museums, theaters, recital halls, the Sterling City library—and the sky-scraping financial district to the south. From the street, the park and surrounding architecture were stunning. From the air,

Sterling City looked like a bull's-eye.

Across the street from the southernmost point of Victory Park sat Silver Bank, a gray stone building that looked more like a small castle than a financial center. It had huge windows and skylights and the sort of peaked Gothic roof that was generally reserved for cathedrals. The glass front doors stood twice the height of an average man, as if the bank were home to an eccentric giant. Normally, it was a bustling building, but on this sunny day, no one dared go near it. Encircling the bank, two streams of purple electricity popped and crackled. Every few moments a tendril of energy arced out and bounced off of a trash can or lamppost, causing refuse to burst into flames and lightbulbs to shatter in a shower of sparks.

Since the electricity had appeared, no one had entered or exited the building. Bystanders who were courageous, or perhaps just foolish, watched from across the street, standing huddled together by the normally cozy benches and planters that marked an entrance to Victory Park. The police, guns drawn, had only just arrived. After an overeager officer ventured too close to the twisting electricity and was propelled backward, stunned and smoking, they were at a loss as to how to handle the disturbance. It wasn't the sort of thing that was covered in training, and, unaware of the situation inside the bank, they were left pacing and sweating under the midday sun, waiting for reinforcements.

On the roof, a tall man stood watchful, keeping an eye out for the inevitable approach of interlopers and police backup. His hands were at his sides, palms wide, maintaining the electric perimeter, ready to raise the streams of energy high into the sky should anyone approach by air. His name was Volt, producer and conductor of electricity. Like every other member of the High Council, the leaders of the modern Cloak Society, he had dropped his given name once he was in his teens as a way of showing his allegiance. His identity belonged to Cloak now.

Volt's trench coat—black, hooded, and reinforced with lightweight bulletproof plates—blew in the breeze, flapping behind him. On each shoulder were three silver bands glinting in the sunlight, marking him as a member of Cloak's High Council. Beneath it he wore black pants and a long-sleeved shirt made of a special material woven of stretchy fabric and ballistic yarn that was both comfortable and protective.

He squinted as the breeze picked up, parting his coat and tousling his short brown hair. Sunglasses were doing little to shield his eyes from the glaring sun, but the slight wind was a welcome comfort. As he brought his hand to the radio in his ear, one of the energy streams below him rose, igniting a low-hanging tree branch in the process. The sound of gasping bystanders caused one side of his mouth to curl up in amusement.

"Perimeter is secure, Shade," he said. "Cameras all fried. What's the situation inside?"

"Beta Team is at the vault," a woman replied. Her voice softened a little as she continued. "Our son is doing well. He took out both guards before they could so much as think about reaching for their guns."

Inside the bank, Shade stood in a uniform that matched her husband's. Dark, bobbed hair came to sharp-looking points at either side of her chin. In front of her stood a cluster of thirty bank employees and customers, who stared straight forward with slack jaws and wide, dazed eyes. They looked like a choir about to burst into song, standing against the western wall of the bank. Shade focused on them, telepathically broadcasting feelings of tranquility to her prisoners. In the past, she had taken delight in listening to hostages panic and beg to be released, but this mission was special: This was her son's debut, and she wanted to be able to observe it without having to deal with any nervous bank tellers trying to play hero. Her brow furrowed in concentration. Her pupils flashed for a moment, turning a bright silver that bled into her irises and beyond, until her eyes resembled polished metal orbs. The sides of her mouth drew together in a loose O as she tapped into the minds of the men and women.

"Sleep," she whispered, a command that would have been barely audible to the hostages, even if they hadn't been under her control. "Forget."

Simultaneously, the group drew in deep breaths. Shade's eyes returned to normal as she pivoted and walked toward her son. Behind her, the bodies fell and crumpled together on the floor with a collection of thumps. A few people began to snore, and the sound resonated through the bank, bouncing off the marble floor and high ceilings.

Alex Knight—fourth-generation direct descendant of one of the Cloak Society's founding scientists—heard none of this. Nor did he hear his mother's boots clack against the marble floor as she neared him. The hostages were the least of his worries. He stood at the south end of the bank—past the rows of mahogany desks at the entrance, and behind the long counter where tellers and customer service agents normally stood. Beside him were his three Beta Team teammates, the superpowered children of Cloak. They wore black pants and long-sleeve shirts similar to those of the High Council but with two distinct differences. The Betas had only two bands on each shoulder, and the front of their shirts featured the Cloak Society's emblem in radiant silver: a skull shrouded in a hood, the bottom of which flared up and around the top of the figure, like wings. Alex barely registered his peers, either. The only thing that mattered to him was the giant metal door of the vault. It was his twelfth birthday, he and his teammates were on the first mission of their careers—Cloak's first public appearance in almost a decade—and things were not going well.

One morning when he was nine years old, Alex awoke to find that everything he saw was colored blue, as if he wore tinted glasses he couldn't take off. Anything he focused on began to glow and pop with a light invisible to everyone else around him. After the initial shock of this phenomenon wore off, he discovered that by concentrating, he could manipulate this blue energy and move things with his mind. His parents called his gift telekinesis and, thrilled by their son's newfound ability, began to train him right away. Now Alex pulled at the door with his mind, arms out in front of him, physically mimicking the action. Sweat trickled down from beneath his wavy brown hair. The door burned a brilliant blue in his mind, but made no hint of movement.

Somewhere inside the vault, nestled deep within the confines of steel and concrete, was the Beta Team's target: a traveling collection of rare gems and metals stored for safekeeping while one of the city's museums prepared for its exhibition. The High Council had taken particular interest in a diamond called the Excelsior, and the Betas were not to return to base without it. The mission was simple enough, but now the vault door towering in front of Alex seemed like an impenetrable obstacle. As soon as he'd laid his piercing blue eyes on it, his heart had sunk. There was no way he could pull it from its dense steel hinges. He was going to disappoint his parents and embarrass himself in front of his teammates.

"Too . . . heavy . . . ," he muttered through clenched teeth.

To his left stood Mallory, who watched her failing teammate with concern. She spoke quietly, but firmly.

"You've got this," she said. "Remember your training. Keep breathing."

Mallory was only a year older than Alex, but he considered her far more mature than that. She was quiet, poised, and above all, focused. Even her hair—shoulder length, chestnut brown—was always perfectly straight, without a single stray lock. This sort of composure was necessary with her powers. With the slightest thought, she could cause the temperature around her to rise or fall instantly, and if she lacked focus, the consequences could be catastrophic.

"Can we please hurry this up? This is getting sad," came another girl's voice, this time to Alex's right. Julie. She stood beside her brother, Titan, their arms crossed as they sneered at Alex. Their identical posture and grimace were the only things that physically marked them as siblings. Julie was the shortest of the team, fourteen, with jet-black hair tied up in two tight balls on the back of her head. Titan stood tall, just over six feet, with a blond crew cut and a muscular build unnatural for that of a thirteen-year-old. Alex made it a point to avoid standing beside Titan when they were in uniform, as his athletic appearance made Alex look scrawny by comparison.

"Seriously," Titan said. "There's no way he is getting us in there. We're wasting time."

Titan's powers had developed early in life, first observed when he snapped the bars of his crib as a toddler. An X-ray showed that the bottom layer of his skin was made up of a flexible, metallic substance harder than titanium, granting him inhuman strength and near invulnerability. He was so proud of his powers that he had completely dropped his real name by the time he turned six. From then on, he was simply Titan.

"Don't listen to them," Mallory whispered to Alex. "Stay focused."

But Alex was feeling defeated. The door was unscathed, and Alex looked as if he might faint at any moment. He could understand why his teammates were frustrated. Though the entrance to the vault glowed with energy in his eyes, to everyone else it looked like nothing was happening.

Quit playing around and get us in there! his mother's voice yelled inside his head, projecting telepathically.

"I . . . I can't," he said quietly, lowering his aching arms. His head throbbed. The door and everything around him returned to a normal dull blue.

He turned to face his mother, and felt he might wither from her scowl. She held her glare for a moment before nodding to Titan.

"Take it down," she said.

Titan grinned and cracked his knuckles. He positioned himself in front of the door, took a deep breath, and began to pound on it with both fists. With each blow, a clang reverberated through the bank, the sound of metal on metal. New dents appeared each time he brought his hands away. Alex leaned against a teller station, trying to rally his spirits and energy. He already dreaded the debriefing they'd receive once they were back at the Cloak base.

Mallory, who had been silently assessing Titan's heavy strikes, stepped up to the door. She placed one hand on it and closed her eyes while Titan took a step back, shaking his thick hands and jogging in place, trying to build up some adrenaline. Condensation formed on the door and quickly turned to frost. In seconds the metal began to smoke at a subzero temperature. Mallory nodded toward Titan, who reared back and placed a single, mighty punch to the center of the door, shattering it. Bits of frozen metal skittered into the vault, where safety-deposit boxes lined a wide hallway and, farther back, a barred gate led to another room where stacks of cash and the Excelsior were waiting to be taken.

"AAARGH," Titan yelled, shaking his fist. "You froze my hand, Temptress!"

"That is *not* my name," Mallory said.

"Oh come on," he said, smirking. "You know you love it!"

"Call me Temptress one more time," she said, placing a

single finger on his shoulder, "and I'll find out what your body's melting point is."

Beneath her fingertip, Titan's uniform began to sizzle. He shrugged her off.

"Admit it," he said, undeterred. "It's growing on you."

"Enough." Shade stepped up beside them. "You have one minute to get me that diamond. Whatever you find after I have the Excelsior is yours."

Then, turning to Alex, she added, "I guess you're not ready to be a part of this team after all."

Her frown lingered, but Alex looked to the floor. Titan disappeared into the depths of the vault with Mallory on his heels. The sound of metal tearing and breaking echoed into the lobby as the two of them tore through the vault's defenses, Titan yelling raucously with every downed gate and door.

As Julie stepped into the vault, her palms lost their color and began to harden and shine. Her fingers grew to twice their normal length, the tips impossibly pointy. By her third step, her hands were now clear, gemlike talons. Arms spread wide, she ran the length of the hallway, slicing open rows of safe-deposit boxes and screaming like a delighted banshee. The contents of the boxes—jewelry, wads of cash, keys, a whirlwind of documents—spilled out onto the floor. She turned around to survey the damage. Grinning, she picked up a ring that housed an emerald the size of a postage stamp and slid it down the length of a claw before racing into the vault's back chambers.

Alex kept his eyes on the ground as his mother stepped back into the center of the bank, one hand to her radio-clad ear. He felt sick to his stomach.

"Heads up, birthday boy," Mallory yelled.

Alex raised his eyes just in time to see an overpacked black bag flying straight for his face. Instinctively, he raised his hands, pushing energy toward the object, causing it to slow and eventually stop, hanging just inches from his nose. He leaned to look past the bag at Mallory.

"Glad to see your reflexes are still working," she said, as Alex released his focus and the bag dropped to his feet.

"Thanks, Mal." He tried to smile. "I don't know what went wrong earlier. I should have looked for another way in. Or—"

"Shh," she replied curtly. She cocked her head to the side. "Do you hear that?"

A noise rose from outside, gaining in intensity. It was the sound of people shouting with joy. Mallory and Alex looked at each other and then to Shade, ready for orders. Cheering was not a good sign for the Cloak Society.

"We've lost contact with Volt," Shade said, briskly walking back to her son's side. She pulled a small gun from somewhere inside her coat. Her telepathy was strong, but only served her in combat when she was dealing with weak minds or was within close range of her opponent. She'd become quite handy with firearms as a secondary means of offense.

"What's the mission status?" Shade asked, turning to Mallory.

The Beta held out her hand. As her fingers unfurled, they revealed a diamond teardrop, running almost the entire length of her palm. Shade's eyes lit up, and she smiled, taking the diamond from Mallory and inspecting it. But the moment of happiness was soon gone, and, zipping the stone into a coat pocket, Alex's mother narrowed her eyes.

Form on me, she said in the Beta Team's minds. *Prepare for Phase Two.*

2

THE APPEARANCE OF
HEROES

A mass of black crashed through a skylight and hurtled toward the floor of Silver Bank. Purple electricity snaked off it, reflecting in the falling shards of glass and casting kaleidoscopic lights onto the interior walls of the building. Alex recognized the energy signature of his father and reached out telekinetically, trying to hold him in the air. But Volt was falling too quickly. The best Alex could do was slow him down before he bounced off the marble floor with a grunt. Alex started toward his father, but Shade made a sharp movement with her left arm, blocking him. Her pupils flashed metallic for an instant.

Titan ran out from the vault, joining his team members. Five bags were slung over his back, bulging with cash.

Julie was right behind him, her body now decorated with bracelets and a tangle of necklaces. Her talons twitched with anticipation. Everyone stared at the new hole in the ceiling.

Floating slowly down through the skylight was a man dressed in clothing similar to theirs, only deep blue instead of black, with white sleeves and white boots. A brilliant gold starburst was emblazoned on the chest, complementing the gold cape that floated behind him as he descended into the bank. He hovered in midair, looking down at everyone over his straight nose and dimpled, square jaw. His hair was full and brassy, swept neatly to one side. The room brightened substantially with his entrance, making Alex squint.

The man's face fell when he saw Shade, but he did not look surprised. His eyes narrowed in a magisterial gaze. The Betas had been warned this man might appear. In truth, they were hoping he would. What they hadn't been told was that to see him in person for the first time would be awe inspiring.

Lone Star—the man with the power of a sun. Everyone in the world knew who he was, had seen him on television before, accepting awards and honors or starring in public service announcements. They had seen him on the covers of magazines or in the news, toppling crime syndicates. But the Beta Team was more familiar with the curses the

High Council spat along with his name and with the way Alex's mother bit at the inside of her cheeks and frowned when she spoke of the threat that he and his cohorts represented to Cloak. Lone Star was the leader of the Rangers of Justice. Like Cloak, they possessed extraordinary powers, but the Rangers were the protectors of Sterling City, the guardians who kept watch from their sparkling tower just north of Victory Park—the young men and women that the media referred to as "superheroes."

People with unusual talents or inhuman abilities were rare in the world. Sometimes they banded together in ragtag teams and tried to emulate the Rangers of Justice, to become symbols of law and peace. But they were hardly ever successful, or even worth reporting upon. As far as the Cloak Society was concerned, the Rangers were the only superpowered people who posed any sort of threat to their goals.

"Lone Star," Shade said, one eye on the shining man and the other on her husband, who was in the process of slowly getting up. "It's been too long. What, ten years now?"

Alex smiled as his mother stalled for time while Volt recouped his strength. It was a classic strategy, but Lone Star was falling for it.

"I wondered how long it would take for you monsters to resurface," Lone Star said, his voice a resonant baritone.

"I'm flattered you made time to come see us," Shade sneered. "Shouldn't you be with the rest of the Rangers, shaking hands and hawking sound bites somewhere?"

"Justice never takes a vacation," he replied. He rested his fists at his hips and raised his head toward the sky.

"Is he serious?" Julie half whispered, half laughed to her teammates.

Lone Star pointed a thick index finger at Shade. The tip blazed with fiery golden light.

"In the name of justice and all that is good, I command you to turn yourself in," his voice boomed.

"How many times do you think he's practiced that line?" Alex whispered to Mallory.

"Morning ritual, I'm sure," she said.

Do not take this lightly. Shade's voice rang through the heads of the Betas. *Phantom will be here to port us out shortly. If for some reason we are separated, regroup at the safe house and travel back to the base using the emergency transport.*

"Guys, look," Titan said, pointing toward the bank entrance. "This is getting good."

Two figures were walking through the front doors, dressed like Lone Star minus the long sleeves and cape. With Volt taken out, the perimeter had been compromised, and Alex recognized these two from the High Council's briefings on the Rangers. The first was Amp, who had served as Lone Star's sidekick for a few years before becoming leader of the Junior Rangers, their version of the Beta

Team. He was a tall African American boy two years older than Alex, with close-cropped hair.

The second person was a girl about Alex's age, with golden-blond hair tied back in a loose ponytail. She walked with assurance, but as she approached Lone Star's side, her eyes were large and darted around the room, revealing her unease. Her name was Kirbie.

The Betas had been anxious to fight their Ranger counterparts ever since they'd first heard such a team existed. Alex smiled widely. He couldn't help but tingle with excitement at the thought of taking out his sworn enemies. The mission was looking up.

"Sir," Amp said. "We've cleared the area of civilians. Thorn is keeping watch outside."

"Good. Now get out of here," Lone Star said quickly. "Meet me back at Justice Tower. This is too dangerous for you."

"But—"

"This is no mere heist. This is the Cloak Society," Lone Star said firmly. "You're not ready."

"Beta Team," Shade said before the Junior Rangers had time to respond. "Show these children who you are."

"Make us proud, kids," Volt said. He turned his attention to Lone Star. "Shade and I will handle this guy."

Lone Star opened his mouth to speak, but Shade was already firing her pistol. Bolts of energy shot through the air, sizzling against his uniform. They left small holes and singe marks, but the man appeared to be unfazed—one of Lone Star's most annoying powers was a seeming invulnerability to physical harm. A beam of light shot from his hand, narrowly missing Shade as she twisted to one side. From Lone Star's right, purple electricity sparked against his side, but again, it looked to be little more than a tickle for him. He remained positioned in the air, calm.

Titan twisted his head to one side and popped his neck with a metallic *ping*. He and Julie had their eyes set on Kirbie, who stood beside Amp, neither of them moving.

"Come on, Blondie," he said, grinning. "Let's have some fun."

Kirbie smiled and leaped into the air. As soon as her feet left the ground, her body began to change. Her fingers stretched, nails thickening and growing to sharp points. Golden hair sprouted from her bare forearms, spreading to her neck and face, where her mouth jutted out, taking on a snoutlike appearance and showing long canine teeth. By the time she reached the peak of her jump, she had fully transformed into a she-wolf.

"Oh crap," Titan managed to mutter before the girl's feet caught him at the chest, forcing him to the floor with such power that the marble cracked beneath his back. She stood on him, leaning close to his face. A roar came from deep within her. Coming to his senses, Titan swiped at the girl, but she was too quick for him, and was in the air again before he could land a blow.

On the other side of the bank, Mallory shot heat blasts at Amp. They flew through the air, clear masses of energy discernible only by their distortion of the air, like heat rising from asphalt, and by the faint sizzle they let off. Amp dodged each blast expertly, rolling and jumping effortlessly. The Junior Rangers had been well taught.

Alex, meanwhile, took cover behind a desk and used his power to hurl objects toward Amp. Two chairs sailed by the young hero. A bag of cash narrowly missed his shoulder and burst open when it hit the opposite wall. Finally a potted fern slammed against Amp's head, causing him to stumble backward, off balance.

"Yes!" Alex yelled. But the junior hero just brushed potting soil off his shoulder and narrowed his eyes at Mallory and Alex.

"You *do* know how I got my name, right?" he asked.

He spread his arms wide, and as he did, the bank seemed to grow quieter. No, not quieter—it was more like the sound was just focused from a single point, seemingly all channeled through Amp, who looked as though he were vibrating.

"Oh no," Alex whispered.

"Boom," Amp said as he thrust his hands forward. A wave of concentrated sound hit Mallory and Alex, who flew backward, smashing up against the wall near the entrance of the bank. Alex's head rang as he saw Julie sneaking up behind Amp, running with her body low to the ground, talons almost dragging on the floor. She jumped, ready to slice the hero across the back, when something stopped her: A frond from the fern Alex had thrown moments before had grown immense in size and wrapped itself around Julie's waist, holding her in midair. With a single stroke, she cut through the plant, but before she could continue her attack, two more fronds were wrapped around her wrists, dangling her above the ground. On the marble below her, the fern's roots broke out of the pot and grew over the bank floor.

"Put me down!" she raged, thrashing her legs about wildly, but the plant refused to comply.

"Go outside," Mallory said to Alex as they regained their footing. "They said Thorn was watching the perimeter. You get him. I'll take care of the plant."

Before Alex could respond, Mallory was shooting more bursts of heat, causing the plant's branches to wither and die. In seconds Julie was free except for a single wrist. She swung just above the floor.

"Watch it!" Julie yelled at Mallory. "You're going to singe my hair."

Toward the back of the bank, Volt and Shade continued their dual assault on Lone Star, who darted back and forth in the air, avoiding most of their attacks. A beam of light shot out of his right hand and caught Volt on the shoulder, causing the man to grunt and stumble backward, his uniform smoking. Alex's mother now fired her pistol while standing in front of the still-sleeping bystanders on the western wall of the bank, sure that Lone Star would not risk harming any of them by attacking her.

Alex wanted to help his parents, but the Betas had other targets. He ran through the entrance and onto the empty bank steps. Civilians and police had cleared out of the area. Across the street, in the park, a boy dressed like a Junior Ranger stood with his arms out in front of him. He was focused on the fight inside via a large window at Alex's left, and his face was rumpled with concentration. Blond and thin, he looked strikingly similar to the she-wolf inside—pretransformation. Thorn. The boy's fingers were moving quickly, and inside the bank, the fern moved accordingly. He was controlling the plant.

Alex was starting down the stairs toward him, when the window to his right shattered. Titan and a ball of blond fur tumbled through, landing together on the bank lawn. Titan's uniform was ripped in several places. Four long gashes in his chest were deep enough to show the glint of metal beneath his outer skin. The girl, however, showed little more than tousled fur in terms of injuries.

Thorn did not seem to notice that the fight had spilled onto the lawn, and was still waving his hands about like some sort of enchanter, focused on the plant inside. Alex mentally pushed him with all the strength he could muster, and Thorn cried out as he flew through the air. He landed at the entrance to the park, sending birds flapping in every direction.

Kirbie turned, hearing the boy's cries, and roared. In her moment of distraction, Titan landed a hard blow to her stomach, causing her to sail backward into the door of a car parked along the street. She bounced off and hit the sidewalk with a grunt, changing back into her human shape, struggling to catch her breath. Titan wasted no time. He ripped a fire hydrant from the ground, sending a geyser of water into the air, and with swift movements he pitched the hydrant directly at the girl's skull. Still unable to breathe, she looked up in fear as the red bullet flew toward her.

But then, just before it hit her, Kirbie was pushed out of the way by an invisible force. The hydrant smashed into the door of the parked car, embedding itself in the metal frame and shaking the vehicle violently. Kirbie stood as quickly as she could, looking around, trying to make sense of what had happened and who had saved her. Her eyes found Alex, who stood on the bank stairs, his right arm stretched out in her direction.

"You?" Kirbie muttered, confused.

Alex stared at Kirbie, slowly lowering his hand. He wasn't sure what he had just done, only that when he saw the hydrant flying toward Kirbie, he felt he had to do *something*. It had been a reflex, an instinct. He had been trained to be brutal in the field—that pulling punches could get you killed. But now that he was faced with an actual mission, he had no desire to see anyone die in front of him.

"What are you doing?" Titan yelled. "Have you lost your mind?"

"I . . . uh . . . ," Alex stammered.

He started to try to explain it to Titan, but something hit Alex hard in the back of the head, and he tumbled down the rest of the stairs. His ears rang. Hustling down the steps was Amp, followed by Mallory. Behind them, inside the bank, flashes of purple and golden light bounced off the walls and lit up the entrance and windows.

Kirbie leaped from the cement. Once again her body began to change, but this time her legs grew shorter and hardened while her arms grew long and feathered. Her boots dropped to the ground, and the sleeves of her uniform receded up the shoulder. In an instant, she had turned into a giant golden bird—a blond falcon. Her wingspan was at least four feet across, and she let out a shrieking call as she flapped her wings and swooped down, alighting beside Thorn.

"Whoa," Alex said, watching the magnificent bird as Mallory helped him to his feet.

Just then their right arms began to tingle and turn

cold. Alex looked down at his palm, where an inky black pool was starting to seep up from beneath his skin. It glimmered, swirling with dark, oily energy, until it formed the shape of the hooded skull on his shirt. The mark of Cloak. Their exit had arrived. It was time to go home.

"Give up," Amp said from the middle of the stairs. "We're obviously better at this than you."

Alex seethed at the Junior Ranger poised like a statue on the steps of Silver Bank. The smugness of Amp's expression made the energy inside him boil.

"My name is Alexander Knight," he said in the most menacing voice he could muster, taking a step forward, concentrating on his enemy. He hoped his mother was watching from inside. "I am a fourth-generation member of the Cloak Society. And you are ruining my birthday."

He thrust his arms to one side before Amp could react, sending the Ranger flying off the stairs, tumbling head over feet onto the grass.

"Let's get out of here," Alex said. The Beta Team hustled up the stairs, their hands throbbing and growing colder with each step.

Inside, it was as if someone had cut two different buildings in half and shoved them together to create Silver Bank. On one side of the room, Lone Star stood six feet off the ground, arms crossed, his eyes blazing with white energy. The area was saturated with warm light, and the hostages lay behind him, still sleeping, completely unscathed. His uniform was riddled with burn marks and smoking holes.

The other side of the bank was draped in shadows, like the light had been completely snuffed out. Volt and Shade stood ragged but not defeated, and above them, floating on what looked like a black cloud, was Phantom. Darkness swirled all around her, making it impossible to tell where her uniform began or ended, and shades of deep blue and purple wrapped around her pale face, mixing in with her snaking black hair.

She raised her gloved hands delicately, and two shadows shot forward. The first was quickly disintegrated by one of Lone Star's defensive blasts, but the other latched around his ankle, pulling him to the floor. More and more tendrils shot forward, holding Lone Star while the Beta Team regrouped behind Shade and Volt.

"You know your powers are no match for mine," Lone Star shouted. "How many times must I defeat you before you surrender?"

"What's the matter?" Volt yelled. "I thought you enjoyed killing our kind."

Lone Star's face sank into a contorted frown. He jutted his chest out toward the clustered Cloak members, and a blast of blinding light surged from his body.

Phantom's lips spread across her face in a chilling smile. She raised her arms, and a great wall of blackness rose around her, absorbing Lone Star's beam and covering the Cloak Society in darkness.

"What about my cash?" Titan yelled. He pointed toward the heavy bags at the other end of the bank, but everyone ignored him. They had what they had come for; it was tucked safely away in Shade's pocket.

Alex took one last glance at the Junior Rangers now running toward them from the bank entrance. Amp was yelling, but over the rush of energy, Alex couldn't understand what he was saying.

With a gust of air the wall of shadows fell over the huddled Cloak members, crashing like a dark wave. It hit the ground, surged forward a few inches, and then sprang back against the side of the bank, seeping into the corners. The Cloak Society was gone.

3

PAST, PRESENT,
FUTURE

Alex felt as though he were encased in ice as he traveled at breakneck speed, freezing winds blowing against his face. Squinting against the harsh air, he could just make out deep purple and blue swirls around him. An unearthly light was shining dully from somewhere up above. He wanted to yell, but couldn't catch enough breath.

This was the Gloom, a dismal plane hidden from the normal world. Phantom's powers allowed her to access the dark place, draw energy from it, and travel through it rapidly. Where others saw shadows, Phantom saw portals into the Gloom, a place she'd come to think of as a second home.

The Betas and High Council all bore marks made up of Phantom's Umbra energy on their palms. It bubbled up to the surface of their palms whenever her powers were in use nearby and allowed her to pull them through the Gloom safely. Still, Alex was terrified that he might somehow be lost in that wretched place. The High Council speculated that one could exist there indefinitely, never dying—purgatory in a cold wasteland.

There was movement in the near darkness, and Alex sensed there was something lurking, watching them as they passed. All around him, barely audible over the rush of air, he swore he could hear animals howling. And something else was odd, too. Something inside him. It felt as though all his strength was being sucked away, consumed by the Gloom. Alex started to panic. His hand cramped painfully.

Then, as quickly as it had begun, the wind died and the darkness was lifted, like a veil suddenly ripped from his face. He was now in the War Room of Cloak's underground headquarters outside Sterling City. The darkness that had brought them there seeped back into the wall, until nothing was left but the normal shadows. Alex wobbled on his feet, feeling half-suffocated.

"Breathe," Mallory said to him. She spoke calmly, but her face was pale. Over her shoulder, Alex could see Julie bracing herself against a wall, one hand to her mouth as she watched her brother, Titan, doubled over beside her. He was coughing and dry heaving. Alex would have enjoyed seeing

Titan look so vulnerable if he hadn't felt so awful himself.

Shade ignored her son, attending instead to Titan. His back and arms were scratched in several places, exposing his metal under-skin.

"Titan," Shade said, putting her hand on the boy's back as he trembled, fighting to regain his composure. "Are you injured?"

"Nah," he said, swallowing hard and standing tall. "Just flesh wounds. Nothing that won't heal in a few days."

Shade smiled and patted his arm. Her eyes glimmered.

The group fanned out. The War Room was composed of smooth steel walls and fixtures above a darkly stained concrete floor. On one end of the room was a long black table, where Julie took off her new jewelry, laying her prizes out so she could admire them in the bright lights. Flanking the table were rows of countertops piled high with blueprints, legal documents, and grid paper. On the opposite end of the room were several large computer screens and stations, and one whole wall was devoted to various guns, knives, and other gadgets and weaponry.

"Beta Team, line up," Phantom said. She tossed her trench over the back of a chair and slowly started to remove her long black leather gloves, exposing porcelain hands. The team was quick to assemble.

"It looks as though you were beaten within an inch of your lives just now," Phantom said. "Who would like to tell me what happened today?"

"Alex wasted our time trying to get into the vault," Titan said, hardly waiting for Phantom to finish her question before speaking. "If I had been on point from the beginning, we would have been in and out with time to spare."

"Are you kidding me?" Alex exclaimed. "You had just as many problems with that door as I did."

"We watched you stand still and sweat for five minutes, and the door didn't so much as budge. I'm the only reason we even got in there," Titan said, banging his hand against his chest. It clanged under his fist.

"I'm sorry," Alex said. "I forgot you could punch through all our problems."

"What's that supposed to mean?" Titan asked. "Why don't you tell everyone about how you stepped in and ruined my fight with that girl?"

"Quiet," Shade cut in, casting a cold eye toward Titan as she made her way to the group. She walked back and forth in front of the team. "It's true, Titan, that the team was able to get into the vault after Alex failed to do so. But it was Mallory's quick thinking that allowed you to break down the door, not your strength. In fact, if you had continued to bang on the vault by yourself, Lone Star would have shown up before you ever took it down. Wouldn't you agree?"

"Yes, ma'am," he said, lowering his head. "You're right."

Beside him, Julie smirked, stifling a laugh.

"And you, Julie," Shade continued, turning her attention to the girl. "From what I saw, you were too busy being attacked by a plant to be of any actual use today."

Julie's face fell and her shoulders slumped as she mumbled an apology.

"We got the diamond," Alex said, more an offering of peace than a fact worth celebrating.

"Yes. And how did you manage to do that?" Shade asked, though she did not pause long enough to entertain an answer. "Through teamwork. Cloak survives because it is a single entity whose livelihood and goals we put before our own. But today you were fighting as individuals."

Heavy footsteps approached from the hallway. The great metal doors marking the entrance to the War Room slid open, and a tall, muscular man entered. His short, dirty-blond hair was pushed back by a pair of weathered goggles. There was a distinct smell about him, not unlike that of charcoal. His name was Barrage, father to Titan and Julie. He was an arrogant man, but with good reason—his powers were unmatched in terms of destructive capabilities. Alex was always awed when he saw Barrage in action, forming small red balls of energy that orbited around his hands before he fired them off in succession, resulting in a series of precise, powerful explosions. With his arrival, all

have up around that place, whatever alarm system or tech they've installed, it's completely foreign to us."

Alex wasn't sure what was going on, but he could tell by the look on his mother's face that Barrage's report was not good news.

"Gage," Shade said, after a brief period of silence, "can you get us past that shield?"

Gage raised his eyes from the gun, which now lay in several pieces on the table beside him.

"The place is coated in an invisible energy shell. Nothing gets in without their knowledge. The force field itself isn't like anything I've ever seen. I don't even know where the power source is coming from, though I suspect it is somehow derived from Lone Star's powers." He paused for a moment, thinking. "Once I have a chance to analyze the data we brought back today, I may be able to come up with a way to break the shield. But with everything else I am working on right now . . ." He trailed off.

"We'll discuss this later. Barrage, were you able to assess points of entry?" Shade asked.

"The twelfth floor still seems like our best option. The observation deck. From what I can tell, it's nothing but reinforced glass behind whatever force shield they have up. It should be simple enough to take out. From there, we could infiltrate both the upper and lower levels. It's not much, but it's our best shot. Gage took blueprints."

"And you were unseen?" Shade asked.

"Lux and Dr. Photon were in Dallas doing charity work. They were on a live video feed with the national news while we were running diagnostics. As for the rest . . ." Barrage motioned with one hand toward the Betas. "Our little distraction kept them busy."

Distraction? Alex didn't know what to make of this. He was glad to hear that some part of their mission had been a success—even if it was unintentional on their part. The others were not so pleased.

"You used us as *bait*?" Titan asked. He started to step forward, but Mallory caught his shoulder with her palm and gave him a hard stare before turning to the High Council.

"We were under the impression that the point of this mission was to acquire the Excelsior diamond," Mallory stated calmly. "And to mark the reemergence of Cloak."

"Today's mission was the first of its kind in almost a decade," Shade said. She hesitated for a beat before continuing. "When you were all nothing but toddlers, Cloak fell to the Rangers of Justice in Victory Park. We were crippled, most of our powered members destroyed, and we needed time to recover from our losses. And to train all of you. Part of today was to see if you were ready for actual combat."

"We know this story," Julie said. "Our mother died in that battle. Why do you think we were so excited to get a chance to fight the Rangers?"

"It wasn't quite as simple as you've been led to believe," Volt said, stepping up beside Shade. "There were certain failures on Cloak's part that led to our defeat."

"For years before the Victory Park incident, we looked on as Sterling City grew and the Rangers treated it as their personal playground," Shade said. "Meanwhile we were skulking underground, carrying out petty missions and forever waiting for the perfect opportunity to take down the indestructible Rangers. Finally we developed a plan to defeat them. We created a secret weapon called the Umbra Gun."

Gage looked up from polishing Shade's pistol, his lips drawn together in a slight frown. The Betas, however, stood enraptured. They had always been told that the battle had led to casualties on both sides and the eventual retreat of Cloak, but none of the council ever elaborated on the specifics when questioned.

"Gage's father created the Umbra Gun and charged it with my powers," Phantom explained. "It took the forces I draw on and concentrated them into extremely powerful bolts of energy, which transported whatever they touched—in this case, the Rangers of Justice—into the Gloom, where they were lost, doomed to exist indefinitely with no hope of escape. We couldn't figure out a way to kill them, but we could get rid of them. And we did. One by one, the Rangers fell, their bodies transformed into shadows and sucked into that dark plane."

"What happened?" Alex asked, completely drawn into the story.

"Lone Star," Shade said. "We underestimated him. Or overestimated the Rangers' moral stance on never killing anyone. It doesn't matter which. In a single attack he nearly wiped us out."

"Facing such terrible casualties, we had to get out of there. We assumed the gun was lost in the explosion," Phantom said.

"Can't Gage just make us another one?" Julie asked.

"The actual gun, yes," Gage spoke up, putting a final polish on Shade's gun. "But my father left no notes on how he managed to harness and concentrate Phantom's powers. It would take years of testing and research to be able to do so."

"It doesn't matter now," Phantom said. "Last month, I felt it: a surge of Umbra energy so strong it could only have come from the gun. It still exists. The Rangers must have taken it to study, and somehow were able to charge the weapon again. It's locked away inside their sparkling tower, waiting for us to retrieve it."

"But can't they use the gun against us?" Mallory asked, ever cautious.

"You're marked with my energy," Phantom said. "I can sense each of you when you are close by on this plane of existence or in the Gloom. On the off chance that the Rangers were brave enough to try to use the Umbra Gun against us and succeeded, I'd be able to pick you out of the Gloom and bring you back into this world almost instantaneously."

"So this is it," Alex said, smiling. "We can finally defeat the Rangers."

"We need a few months to plan," Shade said. "But on the first day of winter, we attack the Justice Tower. We take the Umbra Gun back. This time, the so-called heroes of this city will fall, and once we defeat them, no one will dare stand in our way.

"We're not just training you to be the next generation of Cloak," she continued, looking at each member of the Beta Team. "We're training you to destroy the Rangers of Justice. *You* will be the rulers of Sterling City. And that's only the beginning."

The Beta team stood in the middle of the room with open jaws and wide eyes. None of them knew what to say. They had dreamed of leading Cloak into victory against the Rangers since they had been old enough to say the word "revenge." Slowly, they all began to react. Alex and Mallory smiled as Titan and Julie began to chuckle, and finally laugh.

"What do we do now? When can we know the details of the plan?" Titan asked.

"You'll continue to train normally until further notice," Shade said. "For now, clean up and get some rest. You all have a lot of work ahead of you."

"Gage. Workshop. Now," Phantom called over her

shoulder, heading straight for the door, not bothering to look at Gage, who scrambled to follow after her.

"I'll join you momentarily," Shade said nodding to Phantom.

The Beta Team headed for the door, eager to discuss what was sure to be the most important mission of their lives.

"Alexander," Shade said. "Wait. I want to speak with you."

Alex grimaced at the use of his full name, sighed, and slowly walked back to his mother and father.

"I'll take care of this," Shade said to Volt, patting his arm. "Why don't you go change, and I'll meet you for dinner soon."

"Of course," Volt said. "Happy birthday, son."

He exited, leaving Alex and his mother alone in the room. Shade dug inside her coat for something, and finally retrieved Cloak's newest prize. She held the diamond up to the light, allowing it to cast brilliant reflections onto the floor.

"You know," she said, "when the Excelsior diamond was found, it was the largest uncut diamond in the world. Almost one thousand carats. Can you imagine what it must feel like to discover something like that? To hold something so raw and powerful in your hands? It could have been cut into something truly remarkable, something the world would never again produce. It had so much potential. And then it was broken down into smaller stones that were sold off one by one. This is just the largest piece of it, the Excelsior I. Only seventy carats. A pity, to have something so pure and powerful end up so common."

"Yeah," Alex said, though the diamond didn't look common to him. He wasn't sure what she was leading up to.

"What happened today?" his mother asked, leaning against the edge of the table, her arms crossed loosely.

"Like I said earlier, the door was too heavy," Alex said, the words rushing from his mouth. "I just wasn't ready. If I had been given a little more time—"

"That's not what I meant," his mother said, cutting him off. "The vault was a long shot from the beginning. We're going to have to change the focus of your training from precision to strength. I'm talking about what happened with Titan and the girl."

A moment passed between them. Alex wasn't exactly sure what his mother meant. She had been inside the bank, so she probably hadn't seen what happened. But she was a mind reader, and while he hadn't felt her probing his subconscious, it wasn't out of the question. He thought it best to respond as vaguely as possible.

"She was better than us," he stammered. Then, realizing that this made his team sound weak, he kept going. "None of us expected her to be so fast or so powerful. She caught us off guard, and we never got back in control. Next time she won't be so lucky."

"You pushed her out of the way when Titan attacked her," she said, staring into his eyes, unblinking. Alex opened his mouth to speak, but Shade kept talking. "Don't try to deny it, Alexander. Even if I weren't a telepath, Titan's anger was almost palpable."

"I—"

"Just tell me why."

"I don't know. That hydrant would have killed her."

"Can you be sure of that?" his mother asked. "She's a shape-shifter, after all, and you know how resilient the Rangers tend to be."

"But if she wasn't . . . ," Alex said, floundering for an excuse.

"She didn't seem too concerned about wounding Titan when she was slashing at his chest," Shade said. Her speech was becoming short, her tongue snapping on each word, chewing into each consonant.

"She's just a girl. She's my age!" He was almost pleading now. "I didn't want to watch her get killed."

"She is the enemy. And I guarantee that had your roles been reversed, she would not have hesitated to let you die."

Alex's eyes fell to the floor. Pushing the girl out of the way had seemed like the natural thing to do—the *right* thing to do. But how could he explain this without sounding like a traitor to Cloak? He had trained so hard, had dreamed so often of destroying the Rangers of Justice and making the

High Council proud.

His temples began to tingle and the hair on the back of his neck prickled. His thoughts were jumbled for a split second, like his mind hiccuped. It was a feeling that might have gone unnoticed by most people, but Alex recognized it immediately. He looked up at his mother to see that her eyes were a glossy silver color: pupil-less metal staring deep inside him.

Before he realized what he was doing, Alex imagined a box of blue energy inside his head and pushed all thoughts of Kirbie and the mission inside it. He stared at his mother's cold, lifeless eyes, silently focusing on the box, reinforcing its walls. Suddenly it sparked with energy. His mother had found it.

Shade winced slightly and raised a hand to her temple, as if she'd been overcome with a headache. Her eyes went back to normal, and she looked both impressed and annoyed by the strength of her son's mind.

"My darling boy." She reached out a hand and smoothed down his hair. "This is no game. This is our life. The world may put the Rangers up on pedestals, but they are the cause of all this city's problems. They parade around talking about truth and justice, but what have they really accomplished? They've crippled the city, made the citizens weak and dependent on them. They pretend to care about the people, but all they want is the flattery and praise.

"The Rangers call us villains, but that's just because they don't understand us. They've forced us to stay underground, terrified that we will take over and show the world what poor leaders they really are. When we are in control—and we *will* be in control, make no mistake about that—the people of this city will know exactly where they stand. The strong will join us, and the weak will fall by the wayside. Order will be restored. It's better for everyone, and once the world realizes that, they'll welcome us with open arms. Trust me."

"I'm sorry, Mother," Alex said. And he meant it.

"Today you disappointed me," she said, frowning. "I can't take the risk that your unpredictability will interfere with this attack on Justice Tower. The Cloak Society cannot risk it. Unless you can prove yourself loyal and ready in the coming months, you are off the strike team."

"But—"

"It's not open for discussion. I hope you'll change my mind before the time comes. I want my only son to be there when we defeat the Rangers."

"This is totally unfair!"

Shade narrowed her eyes. Alex slumped.

"Is that all?" he asked.

"You may go to your room," she said, turning her head away from him.

He nodded to himself and walked away. When he was

almost to the door, his mother spoke again.

"Alex," she said. He turned to see that her face looked softer, almost caring. "Do you remember your first lock-picking set? The one we gave you for your seventh birthday?"

"Of course," he said quietly. He had spent countless hours tracing the outlines of the cool metal wrenches and pins with his fingers.

"What did I tell you when you got upset because you couldn't get any of the complicated locks open?"

Alex thought back to sitting on the floor of his room for days, various padlocks and old deadbolts spread around him. He remembered how frustrated he'd become, his fingers and eyes sore from concentration, and how his mother had made him feel better.

"You said I was thinking too hard. To just close my eyes and feel for the pins and levers. That I just needed to believe I could do it."

"Trust your power, Alex," his mother said. "Remember that the next time you find yourself up against a vault door. Or any other big metal problems."

Alex nodded.

"For the glory," Shade said.

"Hail Cloak," Alex replied automatically.

As he walked out of the War Room, Alex's mind flickered with the events of the day. They had retrieved the diamond and served as proper distractions, so Alex could feel good about that, at least. Whatever his future held, he promised himself one thing: He would be at Justice Tower when Cloak defeated the Rangers.

His mother's parting words reminded him of the countless nights in his younger years when she would tuck him into bed, chanting a short poem along with him, calming him as he drifted off to sleep.

For the glory of the Society,
I will grow mighty and strong.
For we were born to rule the weak,
And right a world that's wrong.
Hail Cloak.

4

A VISIT FROM
THE MIST

The original headquarters of the Cloak Society was a Gothic-style mansion built by an eccentric oil tycoon, all dark-bricked spires and stained-glass windows. It looked like a miniature castle compared to the sleek modern homes going up a few miles away. Everyone who saw it assumed it was haunted, which helped in terms of privacy. For the better part of a century Cloak plotted and schemed within its wrought-iron gates. Sometime before Alex was born, they realized how conspicuous and somewhat cliché their base of operations had become and proposed a move to less obvious quarters. In the end it was decided that it was time for Cloak to go underground. Literally.

From there, it was merely an issue of location. Twenty

miles away from Sterling City they found the perfect spot in an area that looked like the backdrop to an old Western film, all cattle fields and barbed-wire fences rising from rust-colored dirt. There sat an abandoned drive-in movie theater—the Big Sky—that hadn't been used for at least a generation. It was located far from the highway, at the end of a long dirt strip of potholes and weeds that had once been called a road. The entrance was gated, and surrounded by tall fencing. A dense screen of trees added to its privacy. Its inaccessible location served as the perfect cover for Cloak's new underground headquarters. The Big Sky was purchased under a false name, as was all the land for miles around the site. Soon, building began.

Back then—before the battle at Victory Park—it was a very different Society. That was when the team was in its prime, and the numerous sets of superpowers made building and installing an entire underground living facility little more than a weekend project. First, the Big Sky was cleared away. One of the Cloak members controlled earth and minerals and was able to move tons of ground with little more than the flick of her wrist. Once the base was in place and covered, the Big Sky was painstakingly reassembled in all its run-down glory. There were only a few adjustments. The projection booth now hid an elevator. The snack bar was equipped with antiaircraft weaponry.

Aside from tech and security updates, little had changed

within the compound since its creation. It was made up of three circular levels that got smaller as they went down, connected by two elevators that ran through the center of the complex. The lowest level housed the War Room, and the apartments and common areas for the High Council.

But it was the middle level that Alex was most familiar with. On one end lived the Gammas—Cloak kids whose powers had yet to surface, and perhaps never would. Not all descendants of the founding scientists developed Umbra powers. Those who didn't served the group in other ways, outside the underground base. They ran for office, took jobs in the media, and were the deans of schools. It was possible, though, for the gifts to skip a generation. Therefore, all children born of a Cloak bloodline were raised in the underground base, where they could both learn the ways of the Society and be watched closely. All the Betas had grown up in the Gamma wing except for Mallory. According to Shade, Mallory was living in the city when her abilities developed. She couldn't control them and a fire broke out, claiming the lives of her parents. Cloak then swooped in and rescued her. Alex had asked his mother on more than one occasion why Mallory had been raised outside the base, but each time his question was met with a pat on the head and the promise that this was a story for another day.

On the opposite side of the middle level, the Beta

Team was lumped together in one wing, with their own private common area and study rooms. The floors were all stained concrete, and the walls and ceilings were shiny stainless steel, which made footsteps echo loudly throughout the long corridors. The living quarters for Alex and his friends weren't especially cramped, but they lacked a certain homey feel. The rooms were designed for utility and function. The walls were all a clinical white, and the lights were fluorescent fixtures that buzzed quietly when turned on. A sink and mirrored medicine cabinet came standard in each bedroom, along with a dresser and nightstand of matching dark wood. In one corner, Alex's twin bed sat unmade, across from a desk covered with a few books, a pile of pens and markers, an open laptop, and a small circus of origami animals that were the result of hours he had spent honing his telekinetic precision.

Alex had tried his best to make the room his own. Tacked to the wall above his desk were newspaper clippings that spanned decades, telling stories of Cloak missions and the resulting clueless police investigations. There were pictures of him and the Beta Team, a few of his parents, and a portrait of his maternal grandfather, Grim. Alex had heard stories of Grim's ferocity, and how his Umbra powers reduced brave opponents to sniveling cowards. His eyes would turn black and glossy, and anyone who looked into those dark pools would see their worst fears play out in their minds, causing them to sink into madness. Grim was the one who had led the charge against the Rangers in Victory Park, and had died for the Cloak Society. His portrait was a daily reminder of Alex's proud ancestry, giving him plenty toward which he could aspire.

Alex was glad to be back in his bedroom and alone with his thoughts. He tossed his Cloak uniform into a corner with the rest of his dirty clothes and threw on a fresh T-shirt and athletic shorts. As he changed, he could feel the tender places on his body where bruises would form overnight. Scrapes and bumps and small cuts weren't unusual for him, or any of the Betas. They were used to getting thrown around in training exercises or while testing the limits of their powers. First aid was one of the skills they learned as Gammas.

Alex sat at his laptop and opened a file that held descriptions of the powers and potential weaknesses of the Rangers of Justice, along with photos and biographical information. All of them looked younger than Cloak's High Council, and had a charismatic air to them that Alex could pick up on even in the photographs. He'd read these briefings many times before, but now that he'd actually *seen* Lone Star, he was anxious to compare his own notes with the text. Alex had to admit that the superhero was astoundingly powerful. If the other two Rangers had even half his strength, Alex could understand why Cloak had had so much trouble defeating them over the years. Lux, the only adult female Ranger, had powers much like Lone Star's, with the ability to fly and produce concentrated beams of light. A few pictures of her showed hair that glowed so brightly it appeared to be white, luminescent, as if stars had been woven into it. Dr. Photon, the third Ranger, specialized in manipulation of magnetic fields and wore thick-rimmed glasses over his dark eyes. Alex wondered if he'd be able to control Titan's metal skin. He smiled at the idea of Titan being forced to dance around like a marionette.

At the end of the file were short descriptions of the Junior Rangers. Alex made a mental note to write up reports to flesh out these profiles now that he'd come face-to-face with them in combat.

He stretched, which made him realize just how sore his muscles were going to be the next day. He walked over to the mirror and inspected a particularly tender spot at the top of his forehead, near his hairline. Thoughts of Lone Star's impressive entrance filled his mind as he inspected his face. Inhaling deeply, he puffed out his chest and pursed his lips, trying to obtain the majesty and confidence that had radiated from the Rangers' leader when he floated in front of them earlier that day.

Behind him came a short, high giggle.

Alex jumped, accidentally letting off a tremor of telekinetic energy, shaking the flimsier items in his room and four members of the High Council were now present in the War Room.

Behind him came Gage, the twelve-year-old technological genius behind Cloak's weaponry and gadgets. He was hunched, an oversized black nylon backpack weighing down his small frame. The Cloak Society had once employed a veritable army of faithful staff and engineers, but the modern High Council found that recruiting and training a fleet of loyal subjects was both impractical and a huge security risk. Instead they whittled down the staff to a few dozen and made do. They were called Unibands, designated by the single stripes on the shoulders of their uniforms. Shade oversaw them, and under her watchful mind, they were devoted to the Society. Gage was one of them, like his father before him.

Gage dropped the pack beside the door and exhaled slowly, stretching his sore muscles and wiping back his black, curly hair. He rested for only a moment before hurrying over to Shade, who was holding her pistol in his general direction. He collected it and, after inspecting the weapon for a few seconds, began to disassemble the gun.

"Barrage, update us on your progress," Phantom said.

"There is no progress," he said gruffly, his voice gravelly and low-pitched. "Justice Tower is completely locked down. We ran every test we could without setting off any alarms, but nothing came back conclusive. Whatever shield they pushing his paper menagerie from his desk to the floor. Standing in front of his still-closed door was a short, freckled ten-year-old girl. Her hand was clamped over her mouth and her green eyes were wide, as if she were wishing she could take back the escaped giggle. A silver headband held back her remarkably red hair, which fell in curls to her shoulders. She wore a black shirt, purple plaid skirt, black leggings, and fuzzy purple slippers.

"MISTY!" Alex yelled, louder than he had intended. "How many times do I have to tell you to knock?"

"How many times do I have to tell *you* that my name's *not* Misty?" she asked, "No one is afraid of someone named Misty. I'm 'the Mist.'"

"What are you doing in here?" Alex asked. Misty had a habit of popping up unannounced and uninvited. "Gammas aren't supposed to be roaming the halls."

"I'm not a Gamma anymore! I have powers!"

"Well, you're not technically on the Beta Team yet either, so . . ."

"It's time people started calling me by my new name," she said, ignoring his statement.

"We've been over this before," Alex said, exasperated. He plopped down into his desk chair. "No good code names start with 'the.' It gets too confusing. It's like having to say 'the Alex' every time you mention me. 'The Alex, make your bed. The Alex, come out with your hands up.' It sounds stupid."

"No," she said in defiance. "It sounds scary. 'No one escapes from the Mist.' It's perfect." She crouched, one arm outstretched before her in a dramatic pose, looking at imaginary opponents who would surely have recoiled in fear.

"You can't choose a name because it sounds good when you recite one rehearsed line. You'll start to sound like one of the Rangers," Alex said. He began picking up the scattered origami animals and putting them back on their feet.

"There's a reason your aunt goes by Phantom now and not the Phantom Queen," Alex continued. "The same reason we usually just say Cloak instead of the Cloak Society. It's too long. People are going to drop the 'the' and you're just going to be Mist. And no one is afraid of mist. You might as well go by Spritz or something."

"Well, it's better than Misty!" she exclaimed.

"Don't blame me! The Mist was your idea. I suggested Smog."

Alex spun back around to face her, only to find that her body was now framed in a thick haze. The edges of her ears and the curls of her hair were disintegrating into the air, hovering around her body, as if she were made up of dust-like flecks now breaking apart.

"Whoa, whoa, whoa," Alex said, raising his hands up in defense. "Pull yourself together, okay? You know I was only joking. 'The Mist' is a great code name. Just don't worry about it right now. In a few years, when you're old enough to be a full-fledged Beta, no one will call you Misty. I promise."

She took a long look at Alex before shaking her head, bringing everything back to normal. Alex was always impressed by the control Misty had over her powers, especially considering what had happened when they manifested. A year earlier Misty had mysteriously disappeared from her room. The entire compound was searched over the course of a few days, until Alex came across a cloud of particles in the hallway that matched the exact shade of Misty's red hair. After analyzing the flecks, it was agreed that the only way for Misty to regain her natural form was by her own will. But just to be sure that no pieces got lost in the compound, Gage constructed a modified vacuum and a large glass cylinder to keep Misty contained until she figured out how to rebuild herself. The High Council called her power "sublimation," the ability to turn from a solid state into a gas. She stayed in her glass container for a week, nothing but a sentient cloud, until Phantom, her aunt and guardian, walked in one morning and found her sitting cross-legged in the tube. She asked for a grilled cheese and lemonade, as if nothing had happened.

Phantom was delighted by this manifestation of powers: Misty had been born to Phantom's sister, who had never developed special abilities of her own. Instead she served as a high-ranking administrator in Sterling City's government, secretly feeding information back to Cloak. Misty saw her mother only a handful of times every year, but the High Council did not view this as a problem. Misty had powers, and it was best that she be kept around others like her.

In the past year, Misty had learned to control her transformation—even to sublimate other objects to travel with her—though she still tended to fall apart involuntarily when she got emotional.

Now Misty's face lit up as she suddenly remembered why she had come into Alex's room in the first place. "The Rangers! Justice Tower! I heard Titan and Julie talking about it. I almost forgot that's what I came to talk about before your modeling poses distracted me!" She was exuberant now, like nothing had ever bothered her. "Oh please, you have to talk your mom into letting me go. I *have* to be there! I can fight! Or I can sneak in and unlock the door! I'll stay in mist form the whole time. Just please, please, please—they have to let me go! Everyone will be talking about it forever after it's over and I'll be completely left out."

She kept talking, but Alex stopped listening. The fact that *he* might not be taking part in the attack had yet to fully sink in. Watching Misty practically burst with enthusiasm made his chest feel heavy. He wanted so badly to be able to celebrate the upcoming attack too. How could he tell her that he had failed so miserably at his mission? Alex frowned as she continued to jabber. His room was beginning to feel unbearably stuffy.

"And then, after we take over the tower, I wonder if we'll get to move there. Can you imagine, living up so high after being underground for so long? With all that light? I bet we'll all get giant rooms. And a pool. I bet there's a pool! Maybe on the roof, with palm trees, do you think? And . . . hey, what's the matter with you? How can you look so sad when we're going to be famous soon?"

"I don't know," Alex said. "I guess I'm just tired."

"But it's only, like, seven thirty."

"Trust me, it's been a long day."

"Oh, okay, fine," she said. For a fleeting beat she looked bored, before the paper animals on Alex's desk caught her eye. "Ooh! Is that a giraffe? Can I have this? Oh my gosh, and this one too? I love this little frog. She's so cute! And—"

A friendly succession of three short raps at the door stopped her midsentence.

"You see," Alex said to Misty, rising to walk to the entrance. "This is how a normal person comes by for a visit."

He pressed the round button on the wall beside the door. There was a click, and the door slid open left to right. In the hallway stood Gage, holding two plates of sandwiches in front of him.

"I thought you might need sustenance," he said. "Peanut butter and jelly."

"If you were a different person, I'd swear you could read my mind," Alex said, taking one of the plates and heading back to his desk. Gage followed him, the door closing noiselessly behind him.

"Oh! Is that one for me?" Misty asked, reaching out for Gage's plate. He pulled it away from her.

"That's quite illogical. How could this be for you when I didn't know you were here?" he asked. "Perhaps you could get your own food at this time."

Misty stared up at him, unspeaking. Alex bit into his sandwich to suppress a grin. Gage was only a few months older than Alex, and he was probably the smartest person Alex had ever met. Unfortunately, Misty had a hard time following him sometimes.

"He means you have to leave now. Go get a snack or something," Alex explained.

"Fine. Be that way," Misty said. She walked to the door with an exaggerated stomp, turning back to them before exiting. "But don't expect my help when you're cornered in Justice Tower and you need the Mist to save you."

Before Alex could respond, she was halfway gone, seeping through the crack between the bottom of the door and the floor, nothing more than a cloud of particles.

"Do you think I could keep her out if I put my dirty clothes up against the bottom of the door?" Alex asked.

"I was thinking more along the lines of reinforced

rubber weather stripping," Gage said. "Or perhaps simply a high-powered exhaust fan."

Alex was glad to see Gage in a good mood. As Cloak's weapons and electronics specialist, he was always busy, evidenced by the deep purple grooves beneath each of his eyes. Alex imagined that with the recent developments, Gage was hardly sleeping at all.

"Doing a little light reading?" Gage asked, gesturing to the Ranger profiles still open on Alex's computer screen.

"Oh, yeah," Alex said. "Although you don't really get what 'sound-based energy' means until you're being thrown across a bank by a sonic boom."

"It's a shame we don't know more about the source of their abilities," Gage said. "It's possible that they have a common point of origin, like Cloak's. Dr. Photon's manipulation of the magnetic field is of particular interest to me, though I doubt I'll ever have the opportunity to examine it in depth."

"I bet he's not even a real doctor," Alex said. "Like he had time to get a PhD while flying around the world taking out mob bosses and wannabe villains."

"Perhaps some small college awarded him an honorary doctorate," Gage suggested, grinning. "He would look good on an alumni list."

They both laughed. Alex tossed the last bit of sandwich into his mouth.

"Hey, you didn't tell me about the whole Justice Tower thing with Barrage," Alex said. He wasn't upset that Gage hadn't told him, just surprised. The two of them had been practically inseparable since Alex could remember. Their relationship disappointed Shade and Volt. While they admitted that Gage was a prodigy, they never viewed his genius as being a superpower. Gage's father had been an ambitious, high-ranking Uniband who had hoped that his brilliant technological designs might secure him a seat on the High Council, despite his lack of Umbra Powers or Cloak ancestry. In the fallout of the Victory Park battle, however, the Society was in shambles, and gadgets were the least of its concerns. Gage's father worked harder, faster than he ever had, desperate for their acceptance. But all he received was an early death due to a careless mistake in his workshop. Eventually, Gage stepped into the role his father had occupied, hoping to honor the man's memory by impressing the High Council. But the young inventor was still only a Uniband, unmarked by Phantom's dark energy, and little more than a glorified servant—a fact of which he was well aware.

"I wasn't informed of the details until Barrage came to my workshop this morning and told me to pack all the analytical equipment I could carry," Gage said. "I was briefed when we were en route."

"I can't say I'm jealous. You smell like a barbecue."

"Yes, well, from what I can deduce, things did not go

so well for you today either," Gage countered. He raised his eyes to Alex. Gage was as good at analyzing people as he was at electronics and machines.

"So you've heard I'm off the strike team."

"Your mother came to my workshop following the War Room meeting with some things for me to look at—analyses of Lone Star's energy she managed to acquire. She discussed the issue with Phantom before the two of them left. Though I'm not sure that any of your fellow Betas are aware of your . . . probation," he said.

"We got the diamond, at least," Alex offered for the second time that day.

"Yes. Its thermal conductivity will prove to be most useful in my recent designs. It should keep the device I am working on from overheating."

"So the Excelsior was for you?" Alex asked. "I thought it was just an easy target. What are you using it for?"

"You're trying to change the subject," Gage said. "Did you save one of the Junior Rangers?"

"I don't know what happened," Alex said. "It was weird. I know that they're our enemies, but I didn't want her to get hurt. To die. Something about her was . . . different, I guess."

"You're talking about her in pretty friendly terms."

"Don't be stupid," Alex said. "It's not like that."

"Alex, I may be Cloak's techie, but I am also your

friend," Gage said. "I'm telling you without hesitation that sympathizing with your sworn enemy will cause you nothing but problems. I've read Shakespeare. I know how this sort of thing ends."

"You're making way too much out of this," Alex said. "You should be helping me think of a way to prove that I need to be on the strike team. This mission is the sort of thing that happens only once in a lifetime. It could change the world."

"The operation is months away, Alex," Gage said. "That is plenty of time to get back into the good graces of the High Council. Besides, strength in numbers, right?"

"Do you think they'll call in the Omegas?" Alex asked. "I haven't seen any of them since before I got my powers."

The Omegas were three superpowered kids who had served as the Beta Team at the time of the Victory Park attack. When their parents were killed in the battle, the Omegas vowed to avenge them. The High Council nurtured this hatred, molding them into covert operatives and turning them into the Cloak Society's first team of assassins. They were then sent out across the country to carry out whatever missions the High Council dreamt up for them.

"I doubt it," Gage said. "The Omegas' greatest asset is that no one outside knows they exist. I'm sure the council will want to keep them off the field as a contingency plan just in case things go awry."

"Yeah," Alex said. "Hey, do you think you could sneak me out of here for a little bit? I could use a few minutes up top."

"Do you think it is wise to break a rule when you're in trouble already?"

"I'll only get in trouble if someone finds out," Alex said, unrelenting. "And they won't with your help. Just a quick visit outside. Please?"

Gage sighed as Alex contorted his face into a pathetic plea. He longed to breathe oxygen that wasn't recycled. If he could just see the sky for a little bit, he knew he'd feel better.

"All right. But only for a few minutes."

"You are the best."

Alex grabbed his electronic wristwatch from the nightstand—his powers wreaked havoc on watches with cogs and hands—and followed Gage. They walked quietly down the hall until they reached the elevator. Gage got off on the first floor.

"I'll take over on security watch for twenty minutes," Gage said as the doors closed. "Be back underground before then."

The first floor housed the Unibands, who had limited access to the other levels. Many of them were well trained in combat should they ever be needed for a mission, but most of them served as caretakers of the compound or errand runners. Gage unofficially led a team of research and development engineers here—the thought being that if there was ever an accident within their laboratories and workshops, none of the higher-level Cloak members would be harmed.

It was just getting dark by the time Alex exited the elevator on the surface, and made his way to the empty drive-in theater snack bar. Posts topped with rusted speakers jutted out of the earth like rows of gravestones on either side of him. As a kid, he had thought the ruins of the drive-in were creepy, until his mother told him to think of it as a movie set, a place pretending to be something else, and from that point on they never bothered him. Technically he wasn't supposed to be outside the base without permission, but he came aboveground whenever Gage was willing to part with his tinkering long enough to help him sneak out.

Alex climbed to the roof of the snack bar, using the old wooden ladder propped up against its side. There, he sat on the building's edge, staring out at nothing in particular. Through one of the missing panels on the old drive-in screen, he could just make out the last sliver of sun setting in the west. Gage was right. The attack was months away. Anything could happen in that time. For now, he could just let his heart race with the excitement of knowing that the Cloak Society's greatest hour was fast approaching.

He lay back onto the roof with his hands behind his head. Above him, the sky was muddled shades of blue, the first stars of the night beginning to appear in the east. He stayed like this as time passed slowly, thinking of Sterling City's inhabitants saluting him as he stood beside his Cloak brothers and sisters. He felt as if he were drifting upward into the heavens, until at last the beeping of his watch brought him back down into reality and back to his home beneath the earth.

5

THE PRISONER'S
DILEMMA

The next morning Alex awoke to heavy knocks on his bedroom door.

"Alex," a voice called from the hallway. In his grogginess, Alex barely recognized it as Mallory's. "Just making sure you're awake. We're due topside in fifteen."

"Yeah, Mal," he called back to her, trying to mask the sleep in his voice. "I'll be there in a second."

I must have forgotten to set my alarm, he thought. Eyes still closed, he reached out with one hand toward his bedside table, groping for his lamp. His fingers slapped at nothing, repeatedly falling on bare wood. He sat up on his knees and rubbed his hands on the wall near the foot of his bed until he found the light switch, causing the harsh overhead bulbs to flicker on with a hum. As his eyes adjusted to the light, he realized that his lamp was on the floor, along with his alarm clock, water glass, and everything else that had been beside his bed when he fell asleep the night before. The cup was shattered, bits of glass scattered everywhere.

This sort of thing had happened before. A bad dream might send his sheets and blankets flying off his bed or push the clutter on his desk to the floor. Alex swept the broken glass onto a sheet of paper with his mind. Once he was sure that no stray pieces had been overlooked, he put everything back where it belonged. The clock was dead. He picked it up and shook it. Something rattled inside its plastic shell. Yawning, he grabbed his watch from the desk and saw that it was 6:53—seven minutes before he was supposed to be aboveground. He raced through his room, changed into sneakers, running shorts, and a black T-shirt, and ran to the elevator at the end of the hallway.

The Cloak Society kept its members in peak physical condition. Cardiovascular health was of particular concern. After all, you never know when you'll be forced to dash through back alleys and side streets to evade pursuing forces of the law. Sure, enhanced durability and stamina are standard issue with most superpowers, but they certainly don't prepare you for uphill sprints carrying bags of loot and weaponry. Under Barrage's watch, the Beta Team jogged five miles every morning, circling the abandoned movie theater parking lot twenty times before the Texas sun climbed high into the sky.

Alex joined his peers, who were stretching in front of the decaying movie screen. Julie's eyes were puffy and her face pale. Titan was on the ground beside her, doing push-ups in a sleeveless shirt and backward baseball cap. Titan put the other Betas' paces to shame. If for no other reason, Alex hated the morning runs because Titan so clearly excelled at them.

"All right, eyesores," Barrage growled at the Betas. "Is everyone stretched?"

"Yes," they groaned in unison.

"Then move out, you pathetic excuse for a team. Show me some hustle."

The Betas began to jog. Barrage followed a few yards behind, barely working up a sweat as the laps ticked away. When Julie began to slow down, he waved a hand and sent a crackling red orb no larger than a dime flying at her heels. It exploded on the ground a foot behind her with a pop, spitting bits of gravel and ash up into the air. Julie yelped and picked up the pace. Aside from Titan, all the Betas, at one time or another, had been forced to go straight from their morning runs to the infirmary on the first floor, where a Uniband doctor treated their burns and scrapes.

After their workout, the Betas headed down to the

middle level to shower and change before breakfast. Everyone was eager to continue discussing the impending attack on Justice Tower.

"I've been thinking about it," Titan said, "and if we split up the city between us, I call the stadium district."

"Why would we want to split it up?" Julie asked. "That makes no sense."

"To make it easier to manage," Titan said. "It's a lot of people, and it'll be easier to keep them under control if we section them off."

"It'll be fine," Julie insisted. "It'll be like having a couple million Unibands running around."

"He has a point," Mallory chimed in. "I don't know that they'd be quite that loyal at the start. They seem to be pretty brainwashed by the Rangers of Justice."

"They'll come around fast," Alex said. "We'll empower the people. Once they realize what an honor it is to be our subjects, they'll forget all about the Rangers. The smart people will realize that Lone Star was nothing but a hack and devote themselves to us."

"Yeah. Who wouldn't want to be ruled by Cloak?" Titan asked. "And if they don't join us, they'll fear us, which is basically the same thing."

"Exactly," Alex said, a rare moment where he agreed wholeheartedly with Titan. "The people of Sterling City will be our army of subjects. They'll help us expand."

"Wait," Mallory said. "So are they subjects or are they a part of Cloak?"

"If they're going to be Cloak members, they've got a lot to learn," Alex said, mulling this over as the team stepped out of the elevator and onto the middle level. "We'll have to set up training camps or something. We'll give out free uniforms. People will love it."

"Just trust the council," Julie said. "They'll figure it out."

"Are we going to have to give them a designated rank? Because eventually we're going to run out of Greek letters," Mallory said.

"Ah!" Julie exclaimed. "You guys, we should *totally* bring back titles! Like nobility rankings."

"Yes!" Titan said. "What's higher, a duke or a baron?"

"Um, archduke maybe?" Mallory suggested.

"Perfect!" he said, suddenly excited. "Titan: Archduke of . . . Titania? No, something cooler than that."

"Sounds like you've given it a full analysis," Alex said.

"Aw," Titan said. "Poor little Alex is sad because 'Knight' is lower on the totem pole than 'Archduke,' isn't he?"

"Whatever we do," Julie said, "I'm definitely going to start a collection of Cloak crown jewels."

"Alex," Volt called. "Can I have a word?"

All of them stopped and turned to see Volt standing in the corridor behind them. Immediately they all stood tall, hoping the man didn't think they'd been making light of Cloak's future.

"Father," Alex said. "Yeah, of course."

As the others continued on to their rooms, Volt spoke.

"Your mother told me what happened with the she-wolf, and your subsequent probation. I just want you to know that I have every faith that you'll prove to us that you deserve a spot on the strike team when we make our move against the Rangers."

"Thanks," Alex said. "I'm going to do everything I can to be there."

"If you want to talk about what happened—"

"That's okay," Alex said, raising his hands. "Too much excitement from the mission and my powers went a little crazy. It was a fluke. It won't happen again."

Volt smiled and pulled something out of his pocket.

"I meant to give this to you yesterday," he said, handing over a photo to Alex. "I thought it might make a nice addition to your wall."

Alex looked down at a picture he'd never seen before. His mother and father, both younger, were huddled around a baby with brilliant blue eyes. All three of them were smiling. He flipped the picture over to find his mother's handwriting. *Alex—6 months.*

"Wow," Alex said. "This is really great."

"You're welcome," Volt said. He squeezed Alex's shoulder.

"You have a lot of training ahead of you, but I'm proud of you, son."

"Thanks, Father."

"All right. I have to go," Volt said. "Time to juice up the generators. Someone's got to keep the lights on in this place."

Volt turned and headed toward the elevators, leaving Alex alone in the hallway. He stared down at the picture for a few moments, relishing how happy everyone looked, before slipping it into his pocket and heading to his room.

Being so close together in age, the Betas were all educated at the same level by the Tutor, a man with the uncanny ability to remember everything that he read perfectly. A second-generation Cloak member, the Tutor single-handedly oversaw the education of everyone at the base. He had done this for decades, and the members of the current High Council were among his alumni. His facial hair was a meticulously groomed black goatee and mustache that had only recently begun to gray, despite the fact that he was in his late seventies. Unlike the other people occupying the underground base, who dressed in dark, monochromatic uniforms, the Tutor always wore earth-toned suits that were a bit ragged in the elbows and smelled faintly of old newsprint.

He rarely left his library, which had grown to occupy

several rooms on the second floor between the Beta and Gamma sections. Even with all that space, many of the Tutor's books and files and research trappings were located off-site. The old man's belongings rivaled the collections of many libraries. The thought of such a wealth of knowledge in one man's head boggled Alex's mind. He wondered how, with the power to recall so many words, the Tutor managed to hold his brain together at all. He regularly sent lists of texts and recordings that he needed with anyone who was leaving the base, and as long as he was kept with a steady supply of new films and scores and literature, he never complained. In fact, he seemed completely unconcerned with anything that happened outside his bookshelves and carefully orchestrated lessons.

The Beta Team might not have been in classrooms for seven hours a day like other kids their age, but their education was intensive. They were familiar with the military strategies of Napoleon and Genghis Kahn and could quote Machiavelli at length. On the day after the bank mission, the Betas spent hours analyzing chapters five and six of *The Art of War*, which led into a brief review of the causes of the French Revolution. They sat on overstuffed couches and chairs, watching their professor at a mobile blackboard, counting down the minutes until they would be freed.

"I would like to finish today by discussing a problem in game theory called 'The Prisoner's Dilemma,'" the Tutor said. "Are any of you familiar with this?"

The Betas looked around at one another, shaking their heads.

"Splendid," the man continued. "I'll give you a hypothetical example, then. Let's see. . . . Titan. Imagine that you and Alex have both been captured by some unnamed enemy and put into different cells."

"Wonderful," Titan murmured, rolling his eyes.

"Your captors give you both the same options: You may either betray your teammate, or remain silent. Titan, if you betray Alex and he remains silent, you are free to leave and Alex receives ten years in prison."

"I'd like Mallory to be my new teammate, please," Alex said. Julie laughed.

The Tutor gave her a stern look. She was immediately quiet.

"Titan," he continued, "if you betray Alex and he also betrays you, you both receive five-year sentences. If you both remain silent, however, you'll each receive one-year sentences. Now, what do you do? Anyone?"

The room was quiet as the team considered this question.

"Are Alex and Titan allowed to speak to each other?" Mallory asked.

"An excellent question," the man said. "No, neither of the captives may communicate with each other, though once the sentences are handed out, they will be able to deduce the other's actions."

Several minutes passed without a word from the Betas.

"All right, if none of you have an answer, we'll turn to our two captives. Titan, betray or stay silent?"

"Betray," he said, smirking at Alex.

"And why do you choose this option?" the Tutor asked.

"Because I'm a bigger asset to Cloak," the boy replied. The Betas groaned audibly. "They'd need me back in action as quickly as possible."

"An interesting choice of reasoning, Titan. What about you, Alex?"

"Betray," he said, glaring at Titan. "But only because it's the rational decision. Whether Titan is silent or not, betrayal is the most logical answer, statistically."

"Correct," the Tutor said. "Betraying, in this case, has what we call 'strategic dominance.' Remember that term as we delve deeper into game theory in the coming weeks."

"It totally doesn't matter what option you choose in our case," Julie said. "The High Council would just break us out. The choice would be made for us."

"She has a point," Mallory added. "This problem is based on the notion that both prisoners are looking out for their own interests. Wouldn't it have to be adjusted for us, since we can assume that neither of the prisoners would turn on the other? And besides, if both prisoners stayed silent, the amount of shared punishment is reduced to almost nothing."

The Tutor smiled.

"Very good points, Mallory. When trust and irrationality are added into the equation, it becomes a fickle problem indeed. Keep these concepts in mind over the next few days. We'll be returning to them very soon. Now, are there any questions before we recess?"

"Actually," Alex chimed in, raising his hand, "I have a question. I was wondering if you could talk to us about the battle at Victory Park. Were you there?"

The others grew quiet, all staring intently at their professor. It was hard for any of them to imagine him on a battlefield.

"Do you not remember?" the Tutor asked, sipping water from a tall glass cup at his desk.

"What do you mean?" Alex asked, puzzled.

"The day of the battle," he said, "you were here, in this very room. All the children were bumbling around on the floor. Once the nanny was called into the War Room to help dress wounds, I was left to watch everyone. I had no idea what to do with you all. I tried to keep spirits up by reading *Le Petit Prince* aloud—in French, first, and then the translation—but you, Alex, were the only one who seemed to enjoy it. Though, looking back, I can't help but think it was perhaps too complicated a book for children who could barely form complete sentences."

"Wait, we were here too?" Julie asked, pointing back and forth between her and her brother. "And we had a nanny?"

Everyone looked confused by this. Alex had been only two years old at the time, so it didn't surprise him that he had no memories of the event. But the nanny posed an issue he'd never thought of before. The current Uniband in charge of the Gammas had also been his caretaker growing up. But she hadn't moved into this position until Alex was five or six. There must have been someone else caring for them before that time, but Alex had no recollection of this person—nothing but a hole in his memory.

"Oh yes." The Tutor nodded to both questions. "She was a wonderful woman, like a governess out of some Victorian novel. This was before the new council locked down security and had most of the auxiliary staff purged. You don't remember her? As I recall, you were all quite fond of the woman."

"No, I don't," Alex said. "When was the staff . . . purged?"

The Tutor hesitated, looking deep into Alex's concerned eyes.

"On second thought, I must be mistaken about timing. My head is so full that sometimes my memories suffer as a consequence. I must have been thinking about your mother's nanny instead. When you get to be my age, things like that tend to run together."

Alex felt that there was something he was missing, some element of the conversation that was being washed over, but he couldn't pinpoint what it was.

Somewhere in the library, a clock began to chime. Titan glanced at his watch and then quickly closed his notebook and gathered his things, bolting for the door.

"Shade's going to kill me," he mumbled. "I'm late for power training."

The others gathered their things and left. Alex caught up with Mallory in the hallway.

"I'm going up to see what Gage is doing," he said. "Want to come?"

"I got talked into braiding Misty's hair this afternoon," Mallory said. "But I'll take the elevator up with you. I need to pick up my laundry."

"Careful, or you'll end up the Gammas' personal hair-stylist," Alex said.

"No way," Mallory said, smirking. "I'd just suggest to Shade that braiding be a part of *your* training."

"Hey," Alex said, "do you remember seeing anything about Victory Park on the news when you were a kid?"

Mallory twisted her face and thought about this.

"No," she finally said. "I don't think I do."

Mallory had been six years old when she came to live at the base, but she remembered very little of anything regarding her pre-Cloak life. In those early years, Titan and

Julie had shunned her because she had not been born into the Society, but Alex had always tried his best to make her feel welcome. Shade attributed Mallory's poor memory to post-traumatic stress. She had probed the girl's mind several times, looking for hints of her past, but never seemed to find anything.

"Ah, well," Alex said, exiting onto the top level. "Maybe it's for the best. I'll see you at dinner. Have fun with Misty."

It was a busy time of afternoon on the first floor, and the Unibands he passed all nodded to him, keeping their eyes to the ground. "Good afternoon," a few of them murmured, to which he responded, "Hail Cloak," without much thought. In a room across from the elevators, several Unibands sat around computer terminals, monitoring the functionality of the base—oxygen levels, power supply, temperature. On his way to Gage, Alex passed the infirmary and a large mess hall, where cooks were already preparing dinner for the nearly fifty inhabitants of the complex. Though the Unibands ate together there on the first floor, the Betas and High Council took their meals in the lower levels, with rare exceptions.

The entrance to Gage's workshop was wide, made up of two sliding sheets of steel. Alex pressed the circular button to the left of the entryway, and the door split in the center, opening with a small rush of air. An acrid electrical smell immediately overtook him.

Inside the workshop, rows of tables and counters of varying heights were piled high with creations of metal and glass and rubber. The area was loosely sectioned off into groups of weapons, utility devices, and oversized projects, which sat at the far end of the room where there were no tables. The size of Gage's workshop was one of the few indulgences afforded to him by the High Council, and even then, only because his work required so much space.

The main workstation was located directly across from the entrance, below a large Rembrandt painting that had belonged to Gage's father, called *The Storm on the Sea of Galilee*. Alex found Gage there in his white lab coat, hunched over a sketchbook.

"Hey, Gage," Alex called when he was halfway into the workshop. "Am I interrupting?"

Gage swung around on his swivel chair, holding a pen in one hand and wearing thick goggles that distorted his dark eyes. His curly hair sprouted wildly.

"Of course you are," he said, grinning. "But I'm happy for it. What's up?"

"Just avoiding my studying," Alex said. "We're starting something called 'game theory' in our lessons, and I have a feeling it's going to give me a headache."

"Oh?" Gage asked, sliding his goggles to the top of his head. They left deep imprints around his eyes. "What problem did he start you with?"

"Oh, no, no," Alex said, shaking his head. "You're not getting me to talk homework. What are *you* working on?"

Gage looked back at his sketchbook. He flipped it shut.

"Just some new weapon prototypes for the upcoming attack," he said. "Nothing special."

"Actually, I was going to see if you had any spare alarm clocks lying around."

"Hmmm," Gage murmured, thinking for a moment. "I don't believe so. Is yours malfunctioning?"

"I had a little accident with it this morning." Alex shrugged. "I think my brain must have hit the snooze button a little too hard, and now it's busted."

"I'll see what I can put together for you later," Gage said, rubbing his eyes.

"Gage, man, you look like you haven't slept in days. Why don't you take a nap or something?"

"I would if there were anyone reliable enough to continue working while I slept. As it is, I think it best that I keep at it."

As he spoke, Alex looked around the room at the long countertops cluttered with electronics and tools. His eyes stopped on a boot poking out from behind one of the tables. He walked over and looked at the floor, where one of Gage's assistants was lying perfectly still.

"Uh . . . is he . . . ," Alex began. "Is he dead?"

"Of course not," Gage said, hopping off his chair and

walking over to the man on the floor. "He's just unconscious. Here, look at these."

On the counter was a stack of red and black click-top
pens. Alex reached out to grab one, but Gage stopped him.

"They appear to be real pens," he said, "made to look
innocuous. I call the red ones Gassers. Clicking one sends a
quick burst of knockout gas shooting out. And these black
ones are Blackout Bombs. They send small electromagnetic
pulses that disrupt electrical devices by causing a miniature
power surge. One can blow a breaker, basically."

"Wow," Alex said, genuinely impressed. "That's incredible. So were you testing a Gasser out on this guy?" Alex
lightly kicked the unconscious man's boot.

"He got one mixed up with his normal pen," Gage said.
"He'll be fine. An hour from now he'll wake up more rested
than any of us."

"I may sneak away with some of those," Alex joked,
nodding at the Gassers. "That way I could shut Titan up in
class. Or use them on him during combat drills."

"Or the next time he's standing at the top of a very tall
flight of stairs," Gage suggested.

The thought of the metal Beta tumbling down an endless
staircase sent Alex into a fit of laughter. Gage smiled widely
and pulled his goggles back down over his eyes, turning
once again to his workstation.

* * *

The Beta Team common room consisted of a few couches and chairs, a large television, and a kitchen area. It was all dark mahogany and brown leather, making it feel more like a hunter's lounge than a rec room. There, following dinner, the Betas gathered at the request of the High Council, anxiously wondering why they had been called together so late in the day. Titan was stretched out on one of the couches, a cold compress on his head. He'd become severely overheated during his outdoor training session that afternoon, and was now whining about it to anyone who would listen, coaxing Mallory over to re-cool the compress every five minutes. Alex stood staring at the wall of movies that the High Council had given the Betas to watch in their free time, mainly old heist movies and period films that involved a lot of medieval conquests and revolutions. Julie killed time by casually tossing throwing knives at a dartboard in one corner.

Finally the door slid open. In walked Shade. The Betas immediately got to their feet, standing at attention, and waited for her orders.

"Good evening, everyone," Shade said. "Don't worry. I haven't gathered you here for late-night training."

"Whew," Titan said, relaxing a little and rubbing his pounding head.

"Despite the failings of yesterday's mission," she continued, "I brought you all a gift. It's last night's newscast. I'm sure you'll be excited to see it."

All around the room, eyes lit up. There was no cable or satellite feed in the Beta Team common room—the High Council kept them up to date on any news from the world they needed to know—so any TV program was cause for excitement. More importantly, they were all keenly aware of what Shade's gift meant: They had been on television.

"I'll leave you to it," Shade said, handing the DVD to Alex. She stood for a moment, soaking in their smiles, before nodding. "For the glory."

"Hail Cloak," they replied.

The Betas gathered around the TV, silent with anticipation, as Alex put in the DVD. On the screen, two news anchors—one male, one female—were seated behind a long, curved desk. Alex raised the volume as the male anchor began to speak.

"Our top story tonight is the shocking robbery at Silver Bank's downtown branch this afternoon," the man said.

The camera switched to the woman. A window popped up over her left shoulder, showing an image of the bank's exterior.

"Authorities are saying no arrests have been made in regard to a crime that resulted in millions of dollars of damage and lost property, including several irreplaceable items that were being held at the bank on behalf of the Sterling City Museum. Police are *baffled* by the apparent mass amnesia experienced by witnesses recovered from the crime scene."

"You guys! This is amazing!" Julie said, before being shushed by everyone in the room. The female anchor continued. The picture of the bank changed to what appeared to be Lone Star's headshot.

"The police department has yet to issue an official statement about the incident, but inside sources say the Rangers of Justice were unable to capture the perpetrators—a rare misstep for the world's most revered heroes. Eyewitness reports from outside the bank suggest that the criminals themselves possessed superhuman powers, leading some to fear that a new supervillain group has roosted in Sterling City. Rumors are already circulating that this could mark the reemergence of the Cloak Society, the criminal organization believed to have been destroyed by Lone Star and the Rangers of Justice ten years ago."

"Of course," a male anchor said, "we would like to remind the citizens of Sterling City that we have every faith the Rangers will bring the perpetrators of this crime to justice. We will keep you informed as this story continues to unfold."

The picture cut to black, and the Betas looked at one

another in silence. Then the four of them began to whoop and clap all at the same time, as if on cue.

"We. Are. Awesome," Titan said, his thick, clanging claps drowning out the others.

6

A CHANCE ENCOUNTER

With their strict schedules of training and studying, the days of the week would have ticked by with complete monotony for the Beta Team had it not been for Thursdays. Thursdays were different. On Thursdays, the Betas and a few members of the High Council would pile into one of the long black SUVs parked in the underground garage that connected to the first floor of the base. From there, they drove through an echoing metal tunnel for several miles and eventually surfaced inside an old barn on the outskirts of Sterling City, on the back lot of Phil's Fill-Up Station—owned, naturally, by Cloak. The place looked like it had been closed for years, but a hidden switch turned on the pumps, which were always full of gas.

If it had been within the High Council's power, Cloak would have been completely self-sustaining—but they still needed groceries and paper towels and soap and coffee and haircuts. There was always a rare book that the Tutor requested or a new tool that Gage needed in order to fix something at the base. And while they could just send Unibands out on most errands, the truth was that spending a few hours in the world aboveground was good for everyone's morale. The members of Cloak couldn't spend *all* their time cooped up beneath the earth. While it's easy to assume that people like the High Council only interacted with other supervillains, realistically, there is no such thing as a villainous hairdresser or barista, and it was far more practical to take advantage of the men and women in Sterling City who would put up with last-minute orders or appointments with no questions asked (for a few extra dollars, of course).

So on Thursday afternoons, Alex and his teammates were left to their own devices in the city for a few hours while the adults took care of business. It was a luxury that each of them delighted in. On the Thursday after the bank mission, Shade and Barrage took the Beta Team and Misty to an outdoor shopping center far west of Victory Park and Silver Bank. The Betas spilled out of the car and immediately lined up in front of the trunk, awaiting dismissal from their superiors. On a lamppost beside their vehicle, a large metal sign read:

HIDE YOUR BELONGINGS, LOCK YOUR DOORS, TAKE YOUR KEYS.
—A FRIENDLY REMINDER FROM THE RANGERS OF JUSTICE

"Ugh," Titan groaned as he pointed the sign out to his sister. "I have a friendly reminder about how we're going to beat them to a pulp the next time we—"

Shade cleared her throat, and the metal boy fell silent.

"Remember," Barrage said. "You are Cloak, but you're also in public. We don't need any unplanned incidents calling attention to us prematurely. Behave yourselves if you want to continue to enjoy the privilege of Thursdays."

They all knew what this meant: It was an order to blend in. Alex understood the necessity of reminding everyone to keep a low profile, but they all knew better than to use their powers in public or so much as breathe the word "Cloak." And while anyone who spoke to Titan might think him obnoxious, Alex hardly thought anyone would suspect him of being an actual supervillain in training. Sterling City was home to several million people, not to mention the countless tourists. It was easy to be another face in the crowd.

"All right," Shade said. "Mallory has a radio if there is an emergency. We'll pick you up right over there at the side entrance in two hours. Don't be late."

As they departed from the parking lot and headed to

explore the shopping center, Shade's voice sounded in Alex's head.

Keep an eye on Misty today. She is your responsibility.

Before Alex could respond, Shade was back inside the SUV.

I'm being punished, Alex thought. He turned to see Misty standing behind him with a wide grin on her face. Obviously she knew that Alex was her keeper for the afternoon. She grabbed his hand and pulled him toward the shopping center along with the rest of the Betas.

"Ice cream! Let's get ice cream sundaes first! It's so hot out here," she said. As she dragged him along, Alex tried desperately to remove his hand from her grip. "Oh! I bet they have a big shoe store here. So after we eat our ice cream, we can go look at shoes! The Unibands are never any help when we go look at shoes, but I bet you will be much better at it."

"That can't be true," Alex said. "I only see one color, so how can I . . ."

But she wasn't listening, and continued to plan their afternoon. By the time they actually reached the shopping center, Misty had mapped out a schedule that they would never be able to complete in their two hours of freedom.

Usually Alex and Mallory spent their Thursdays together, but Misty was determined to find ice cream, and Mallory's first stop of the day would be a lengthy trip to the bookstore as she gathered materials that the Tutor had requested. So, hesitantly, Alex set off into the bustling shopping complex with Misty. He had to admit that ice cream did sound good.

They found an ice-cream shop a third of the way through the shopping center. Inside, the line was long, but the air conditioner was blasting at full strength, so Alex didn't mind. Kids ahead of him furrowed their eyebrows as they tried to decide on a flavor. Alex smirked. He wondered what it was like to be carefree, to worry about such insignificant decisions. *How weak,* he thought.

Misty decided on cotton-candy-flavored ice cream covered with chocolate chips, whipped cream, and three different varieties of sprinkles. Alex ordered plain chocolate for himself. Single scoop.

As Alex paid, Misty looked for a table. The place was busy, full of kids done with school for the day. She couldn't see an empty table, but she did find two empty seats at a booth with four other girls, so Misty decided to make new friends.

"Hi!" Misty said to the girls.

The group stopped talking and stared at the red-haired kid in front of them. No one spoke. Then, completely ignoring her, they turned back toward one another and continued talking.

"I like your outfits!" Misty continued, not dismayed.

Again the girls ignored her, but Misty stood her ground.

"What are you drinking? This is a cotton candy sundae. It's really good! Do you want to try it?"

"Oh my gosh, y'all," one of the girls said. "Who is this kid?"

"Seriously, don't you have any friends your own age you can go play with?" the one closest to Misty asked.

"Well . . . no. Not really. I mean . . . Alex is here, but he's a few years older, so . . ." Tears started welling up before Misty could stop them. The edges of her body began to atomize, outlining her in a subtle blur.

Alex, catching sight of her atomizing red hair, dashed over and placed his hand on Misty's back, quickly leading her away from the table. Behind him, the girls laughed.

"Hey," he said to Misty, "calm down. Are you okay? Do you want to go look at shoes?"

"What's the point?" Misty said, her eyes still on the girls. "No one is going to see them but you and the people at the base anyway."

"Hey. Watch this," Alex whispered to Misty, winking.

He looked back at the girls. His eyes narrowed as they landed on a tall cup at the center of the table. It glowed a brilliant blue in his vision, and suddenly the bottom of the cup crumpled, sending bright red liquid high into the air, coating everyone at the table.

Misty gasped and smacked Alex's stomach as the girls all screamed.

"Alex!" she said. "You're going to get us in trouble!"

"Don't worry about it," he said, pushing her again toward the exit. "This will be our little secret."

Misty raised her head with a satisfied grin and walked outside.

As they stood eating their ice cream, Alex looked around for their next indoor, AC-filled destination. Toward the end of the mall, he spotted a sign that jumped out at him: GAMEMASTER, it read in bright blue letters.

"I think I see an arcade over there," he said. "How about we go play some games, huh?"

Misty needed little in the way of encouragement. As soon as her eyes landed on the sign, they were off again, jetting toward the storefront, set back from the main shopping complex in a long breezeway. Inside, the arcade was noisy and full of flashing lights. It was a large, open room, stocked full of everything from stuffed-animal crane machines to the newest virtual reality simulators.

"Over here! Let's get some tokens," Misty called to him, having found the cash machines.

They changed some money, and Misty tried to convince Alex to join her in some dance game that caught her eye. After a few whining pleas, she handed her ice cream over to Alex and hopped onto the machine alone, quickly becoming so engrossed in mimicking the moves on the screen that she hardly noticed Alex was there at all.

The entrance to the arcade swung open as more gamers came inside. Through the open door, Alex heard people shouting in the center of the shopping complex. Immediately he worried that Julie or Titan had picked a fight and were making a scene. He rushed out into the breezeway and jogged toward the commotion.

A tall man rounded the corner running at a full sprint, carrying something bulky under his right arm. He was looking back over his shoulder, completely unaware that Alex was directly in his path.

"Whoa, hey—," Alex started, but it was too late, and the two of them collided, both tumbling onto the concrete. Alex's shoulder rammed into the brick side of the breezeway, and his and Misty's ice creams splattered on the ground.

"Dude," Alex said as he began to pick himself up. "Watch where you're going."

The man lay on the cement, moaning. The parcel he'd been carrying under his arm had been flung several feet away from him. Alex now recognized it as a purse—he'd accidentally run into a bag snatcher. He heard approaching footfalls as a female voice rang out.

"You there! Stop! In the name of . . ."

As the girl attached to the voice ran into the breezeway, Alex's eyes widened. Kirbie.

". . . justice," Kirbie whispered. She was dressed in a light T-shirt and shorts, her flip-flops in one hand.

"Oh no," Alex said.

Kirbie jumped back and took a defensive stance, flexing her arms in front of her as she stared at Alex incredulously. Her features were changing, her nails and fingers beginning to extend as her ears drew back and her eyes became more diamond shaped. She was flirting with transformation, ready to take her wolf form and attack at a moment's notice. She could hear the bystanders whispering to one another.

"Who's that girl?"

"I think she's one of the Junior Rangers."

"No, no. This girl's just a kid."

"Well, yeah. That's why they're called *Junior*."

"I wonder what she can do. Is that boy one of them too?"

Kirbie glanced at the man on the ground, who was still whining, and then brought her attention back to Alex.

"What are you doing here?" she asked. It sounded more like a command than a question.

"What are *you* doing here?" Alex needed to get back to Misty, and find the others to warn them that the Rangers of Justice were in the shopping center. He just needed to figure out a way to get away from Kirbie.

"I was trying to go shopping," she snapped. "But now I'm chasing bad guys. Making sure people like you don't cause any problems."

Being compared to the man on the ground was insulting to Alex. They might have both been classified as thieves— even as "bad guys"—but they were leagues apart. A man like the mugger had no dignity, no finesse. As far as Alex was concerned, Kirbie was lumping diamonds with dirt just because they both came from the ground. Still, knowing that she was out shopping meant that Kirbie might be alone, which was all the better for Alex.

"That guy will be up and trying to get away soon," he said. "You'll probably want to—"

"He just stole a purse," she countered, her voice low so as not to alarm anyone in earshot. "He didn't rob a bank with his supervillain friends."

"I wouldn't call them all my *friends*, exactly." Alex was stalling for time, weighing his options. If she was alone, he might have a chance of defeating her. But using their powers in public was strictly off-limits for the Betas. They risked exposure as Cloak members and incarceration, which would then force the High Council to plan a jailbreak—a tedious and time-consuming annoyance.

"Where are they?" Kirbie asked, realizing the high probability that more Cloak members were lurking around the mall—that the purse snatcher had just been a ruse to lead her into a trap. "Where are your teammates?"

"They aren't here. I swear. I just came for ice cream," Alex said quickly, gesturing to the sticky mess on the ground beside him where he'd fallen. He didn't want to give her any reason to call in reinforcements.

"Right. Why should I believe anything that comes out of your mouth?"

"Because—"

"Why am I even talking to you? I should just—"

"Because I—," he stammered, interrupting her. "I kinda saved your life a few days ago."

The words hung in the air between them, floating somewhere between a question and an admission. Kirbie opened her mouth to speak, but hesitated. She stared back at him in silence, her eyes narrowed and eyebrows pushing toward each other, analyzing Alex's face. She dropped her arms, exhaling, finally lowering her guard, if only a little.

"So that *was* you," she said.

"Yeah," he said. "That was me."

"Why? How?" She stumbled over her words, unsure of which question was more important to her.

Alex glanced around. The crowd seemed to have grown bored and was beginning to disperse back into shops, where the air was cooler. The man on the ground, too, was on the move, finally recovered from his fall and trying his best to creep away unnoticed. Alex smirked.

"Telekinesis," he said. "I can move things with my mind. Here, watch."

He focused on the mugger, watching him crackle with blue energy, and gave a hard mental push. The man, who was beginning to stand, went sprawling back to the ground with a groan. Kirbie took in a sharp breath as she watched, then, seizing the moment, rushed over to the man. From her back pocket she produced two long plastic ties, which she used to bind the man's hands behind his back. Alex started to back away.

"Don't you dare move," Kirbie said to Alex, standing with one foot on the mugger's back.

"You don't want to fight me here," Alex said. "Not with all these people who could get hurt."

"I can't just let you leave."

"You kind of owe me," Alex retorted. If he could just get away and find Mallory, she'd know what to do.

"Why?" she asked. "Why did you push me out of the way of that hydrant? I'm your enemy."

"Well . . . ," Alex started, but he didn't have an answer. For the past few days, he'd tried to forget about the whole thing, focusing instead on how he'd make it back onto the strike team. He'd saved her on impulse, but that was hardly an answer, and admitting that might make her think he and his teammates were weak. Still, he had to tell her something.

"Because I'm thinking of leaving the Cloak Society," Alex lied. He didn't realize what a perfect excuse this was until after the words had left his mouth. Not only did this explain his previous actions, but it made her lower her guard even more. After all, nothing would improve the Rangers' image more than rehabilitating a supervillain.

"Oh," Kirbie said, taken by surprise. "That's wonderful. You should come back to Justice Tower with me then and talk to Lone Star or—"

"No!" Alex said quickly. "I, um . . . I'm just really confused right now." They stared at each other, neither of them sure what to do or say next.

"I have to take him to the police," Kirbie said, motioning to the mugger. She looked at Alex skeptically, unsure what to make of this turn of events. "If you're thinking of leaving Cloak, I'm sure the Rangers can find a way to help you."

"Thanks," Alex said. Relief washed over him that she was leaving.

"I'm patrolling Victory Park this weekend on the night shift," she said. "If you need someone to talk to . . ."

Alex said nothing, but nodded. Kirbie pulled at the mugger's arms, trying to force him to stand. He resisted and cursed her. A low growl came from her throat, and the man complied. She turned to look at Alex one last time.

"I'm not stupid," she said. "I've got incredible senses in my animal form, and I'll know if you're not alone. If you show up with your friends, I'll call in the Rangers and we'll put you away. I promise."

Alex started to respond, but the girl was transforming. Her clothes strained against her now feathered form, the sleeves of her T-shirt snapping open at the seams. Before the mugger could so much as scream in shock, Kirbie's falcon talons picked him up by the shoulders and flew him out of the breezeway. She was gone.

Alex ran back into the arcade, where Misty was exactly as he had left her, a handful of kids her age now cheering her on over the game's techno beats. Alex stood, watching Misty work through song after song until he was certain Kirbie would be long gone. Nevertheless, he kept one eye on the arcade entrance.

"All right, Misty," he said curtly, glancing at his watch. "Time to go."

Misty was reluctant to leave all the admiration and thumping speakers, but the last thing she wanted to do was be late for their pickup. Besides, Alex had a grave look on his face. The two of them walked toward the parking lot in silence. With each step, Misty wanted to ask what the matter was, but she was frightened by Alex's severe expression. They were the last to arrive at the SUV. The adults were in the front, where Shade sat in the driver's seat, air conditioner on full blast. Julie was in the far back beside Titan, the boy's head against the window, eyes closed. Alex slid in next to Mallory in the middle row.

"You look flushed," she said.

"Yeah," Alex said. "It's like a hundred and ten out there. How was your afternoon?"

"This one picked a fight with some older boy who offered to buy me coffee," she said, jerking her head toward Titan.

"I could have taken him," Titan said, not bothering to open his eyes.

"Of course you could have," she said. "Your body is made of metal. I was afraid if you threw a punch, you'd break his nose."

"That was no reason to go all frosty on my head!" Titan complained. "I've had a brain freeze for an hour now, Temptress."

"That is *not* my name," Mallory said, her voice rising along with the temperature around her. She took a slow breath, and calmed down.

Alex had been debating whether to tell anyone about his encounter with Kirbie. Technically, it was his duty to report the incident to the High Council. There was no reason not to—he'd managed to avoid fighting her or getting arrested, after all. But he was in enough trouble because of her already. What if the council blamed him for being careless or punished him for not figuring out a way to take her hostage? Or worse, what if his mother poked around in his mind and heard the things he had told her? However untrue they were, she would be furious.

No, he thought, he would just keep the whole afternoon to himself.

"Oh hey, I got this for you," Mallory said, reaching into a shopping bag at her feet. "Happy birthday. I thought you might need a target for weapons training."

She pulled out an action figure encased in plastic and cardboard and handed it over to him. LONE STAR, the packaging said in big gold letters. FULLY ARTICULATED, WITH SUPERHEROIC LIGHT POWERS! Sure enough, there he was—a grinning, six-inch plastic likeness of the man they had faced days before. Alex mouth fell open.

"I think these are collector's items," Mallory said. "I had to fight a little boy to get this."

"Amazing," Alex said, grinning. "This is awesome. Thanks."

"Everyone in? Everything okay?" Shade called from the front of the car, her eyes in the rearview mirror.

"Everything's great," Alex said. "Let's go home."

7

FAMILY
DINNER

"This is so lame," Julie said, drumming her fingers on the table.

"It's called team building," Mallory said. "And it's an order."

"Relax," Alex added. "Would you really rather be running drills outside?"

The three of them stood at a square table in the Gamma common room, on the middle level of the base. The place was markedly different from the rest of the complex. It was carpeted, painted a soft, peaceful green, and was complete with all the normal trappings of a kid's play area—beanbags, puzzles, lock-picking kits, and emergency tranquilizers should any of the kids suddenly develop dangerous superpowers. On the other side of the room were almost a dozen children younger than Misty, most half her age. They stood in line, waiting with excitement for Titan to lift them high over his head with one arm.

"Alex, how do you want me to do this?" Mallory asked, picking up a pitcher of water.

"Um," Alex murmured. "Just slowly pour it and I'll catch it."

Shade had given the Betas a simple task in order to promote teamwork and to impress the Gammas: making snow cones. Mallory held the pitcher over a large bowl in the center of the table and started to pour. The liquid inside fell a short distance, then began to pool in midair. Soon the entire contents of the pitcher floated before them. Alex raised his hands and rotated them, causing the floating puddle to shift and form a ball. Mallory reached out with one finger, skimming the surface of the water, and immediately the ball hardened into ice.

"You're up, Julie," Alex said. "I'll just hold it over the bowl until you're done."

Julie sighed and let her fingers hands harden and morph, until her clear talons were fully formed.

"I thought you were transforming up to your elbows now," Mallory said.

"I *can*," Julie said, annoyed. "But it takes a lot of energy and concentration. I'm not about to waste that on this."

She placed her hands on either side of the ice ball and began working her fingers back and forth over the surface in rapid movements. A high-pitched, scissorlike sound filled the air as fine shavings of ice collected in the bowl below.

"We should be practicing against android versions of the Rangers or something instead," she said. "Can't Gage whip up a robotic Lone Star?"

"I don't know what you're complaining about," Alex said. "This is easy work."

"I'm just not a big kid person," Julie said.

"Your brother doesn't seem to mind them," Alex said.

On the other side of the room, Titan trudged slowly across the floor as half a dozen Gammas hung from his arms and legs, trying without success to slow him down. With every step forward, they giggled in delight.

"They love him," Mallory said. "It's like he has his own miniature fan club down here."

"He must have hit his head during the bank mission," Julie said. "I don't know how he puts up with them."

"Maybe they connect on an intellectual level?" Alex asked.

Mallory smiled widely, and in spite of herself, Julie chuckled.

"I heard that," Titan said, shooting Alex an angry look.

"It was a compliment," Alex said, smirking. "Some of these Gammas are really smart."

"I'm just looking forward to the day when they're all powered, so I don't have to count on a weakling like you to watch my back," Titan sneered. Then he turned his attention back to the kids, teasing them. "You'll never be Betas like this! Better put some muscle into it or the Rangers will come and get you."

"Tell us what it was like to fight the Rangers!" one of the Gammas exclaimed. "Were they scary?"

"Are you kidding?" Titan asked. "Do you think those losers are anything compared to the Cloak Society? No way."

"Did they try to kill you?" another asked.

"Of course they did," he said. He raised his arms—and the attached Gammas—into the air and clenched his fingers maliciously. "They were monsters! There was one who turned into a giant werewolf, with long fangs and claws and a *vicious* roar. But do you think she was any match for Titan?"

"NO!" the kids squealed.

"I can't wait to be old enough to fight them," said one little boy.

"Did you kill the werewolf?" asked another.

"Well," Titan said, crouching down as the Gammas gathered close, "it was easy to defeat her. The werewolf begged me to let her live, and I told her that Cloak has *no* mercy for those who would oppose us. But since I was feeling nice, I let the big bad wolf go so she could tell the rest of

Sterling City that the Cloak Society is on its way."

"Whoa!" a little girl said.

"You know, you kids are very lucky," Titan said, suddenly getting serious. "By the time you're Betas, we'll have taken over, and you'll have an entire city to play in. Who knows—maybe an entire *state* by then."

"Really?" a Gamma asked loudly over the incredulous whispers of the others.

"Of course," Titan said, smiling brightly. "You kids are the future of Cloak. Just by being born one of us, you're already better than everyone else in this world."

Alex's stomach clenched once Titan mentioned Kirbie. He'd hardly dared think of his encounter since they'd left the shopping center. But now, standing in the Gamma room he'd once called his own playroom, he couldn't help but feel that he hadn't acted like a true Cloak member should have. Maybe he could have quietly captured her. At the very least, he should have told the council everything. But it was too late now. He closed his eyes and breathed deeply, trying hard to push these thoughts from his head.

A girl several years younger than him ran up to Julie, staring wide-eyed as the Beta's swift talons demolished what remained of the ice ball.

"Wow," the Gamma whispered, drawing out the word. "Your nails are so pretty!"

"I have an excellent manicurist," Julie said flatly.

"When I have powers," the girl continued, "I hope they're cool like yours."

"If you *get* powers," Julie muttered as the last of the ice ball fell into the bowl. Alex glared at her.

"I will," the girl said, her face falling slightly. "I wish and wish every night that I'll get to be a Beta one day."

"If you are truly devoted to Cloak," Alex said, trying his best to cheer the girl up, "I bet you'll end up with a power that's better than all of ours."

Jamie, the Uniband in charge of taking care of the children, entered from the hallway. She had a gentle face and short blond hair, and Alex smiled as she approached. In his final years as a Gamma, Jamie had watched over him, and he'd always liked her. In fact, it was possible that she was the only Uniband in the entire base whose name he knew—aside from Gage, whom he always considered to be an honorary Beta, despite what his parents thought. Jamie's presence now, though, reminded him of the Tutor's comments earlier in the week, and how he couldn't remember who his nanny had been prior to her.

"Thank you all for doing this," Jamie said, setting a bottle of bright purple liquid and a stack of paper cups on the table beside the bowl now piled high with ice shavings. "They always get so excited when they get to interact with the Beta Team."

"All right, everyone," Mallory said, her hands cupped

around her mouth. "Come and get them!"

In unison, the Gammas turned their heads, then stampeded toward the table.

"Whoa, whoa, whoa," Jamie said. "One at a time. Tony, you can go first, since you were the only one who could name all our founding scientist forefathers this morning."

A boy with curly brown hair pushed his way to the front of the line, anxious for a treat.

"You're getting so big, Tony. I hardly recognized you," Alex said, picking up a cup and packing a handful of shaved ice into it. "I hope you like grape."

"Um, Alex . . . ," the boy said. "Do you think you could use your powers to do it instead?"

Alex smiled and wrapped his thoughts around the cup, making a show of packing the ice and pouring the flavored syrup in. Soon all the Gammas were eating and laughing through purple lips.

"Now, what do we say to our Beta Team brothers and sisters?" Jamie asked.

"Thank you!" the Gammas yelled.

As the Betas cleaned up, the entrance to the playroom slid open. Phantom walked in, trailed by Misty.

"Hi," Misty said, but her voice was soft, lacking the chipper energy it usually had.

"Are you okay, Misty?" Alex asked. "You look a little pale."

"She's just tired," Phantom said. "We've been testing her powers this afternoon, and she's all tuckered out."

Misty nodded, glancing around as if in a daze. It looked to Alex like she might fall asleep standing there in front of them.

"Did everything work out here?" Phantom asked. "Any problems?"

"None, ma'am," Mallory answered.

"Wonderful," Phantom said. "I'm going into the city to pick up dinner. I assume everyone would be happy with pizza."

"You're going into the city?" Misty asked, perking up, her eyes growing large. "Will my mom be there? Will you bring her back with you? Could I—"

"Darling," Phantom said, patting her head. "Your mother is very busy helping us in the city. I'm sure she'd love to come see you, but she just doesn't have the time at the moment. But you know what would make her very happy? If you got a good night's sleep and trained really hard tomorrow so that you are helping out Cloak as much as she is. All right?"

"Okay," Misty said, her eyes falling to the floor.

"Let's get you tucked in right away. You look exhausted."

Misty nodded drowsily. Phantom motioned to Jamie, who swept in and guided Misty to the door and off toward her room.

"Any requests?" Phantom asked.

"Supreme," Titan said. "Extra large. I'll eat a whole one."

"I'm sure you will," Phantom said, turning to leave. "For the glory."

"Hail Cloak," the Betas and Gammas said in unison.

The Beta Team and the High Council gathered every Friday night for a big dinner brought in from Sterling City, meeting in the formal dining room on the base's lowest level. They sat at a dark table long enough to seat thirty—a relic from the days of a larger Cloak roster. At the head of the table, the Cloak Society's skull emblem hung on the wall. It was as tall as Alex, molded out of brilliant silver.

At seven o'clock, Phantom walked out of the shadows of a huge fireplace at the other end of the table, her arms piled high with cardboard boxes that were quickly spread out and surrounded by the Betas.

Titan's plate was stacked high with food. He took a slice off the top and moved it toward his mouth. Then, pausing, he held it out to Mallory, giving her an exaggerated puppy-dog face. Traveling through the Gloom had taken some of the heat out of the pizza. Mallory rolled her eyes but traced her hand over the top of his slice, causing the cheese to bubble and darken. Titan smiled and devoured it ravenously.

"Titan," Barrage said, "this may just be pizza, but eat with dignity, son."

"Alex," Volt said, "would you pass me some red pepper?"

"Of course," Alex said, focusing on a packet lying on the table and floating it toward his father.

"You should have seen the Gammas today," Phantom said to the rest of the council. "They all have a renewed sense of excitement and pride after spending time with our Betas. They can hardly wait to don a Cloak uniform."

"Just wait until we tell them about how we defeated the Rangers in their own base," Titan said through a mouth full of pizza. "We'll be their *heroes*."

"Word choice," Julie said.

"Titan's right," Shade said. "You will be heroes to them and to the rest of Sterling City. They only call us super-villains because they don't understand what honor it will bring them to serve under us. And when the history books are written, they'll mark all of you as the champions who brought order to the city. The Rangers will be nothing more than a footnote."

"What was it like to defeat so many of the Rangers?" Mallory asked. The room got very still as the Betas eagerly awaited a response.

"I wish you could have seen their faces when the first of their kind fell," Shade said. "Fear. For the first time, they were afraid. We'd been playing the same game for decades: thwarted plans, arrests, jailbreaks. In combat they had always bested us, never falling without rising again. Whenever you thought they had taken their last breaths, they pulled themselves together and saved the day. So to see the first of their own disappear like that . . . it was unimaginable to them. The Rangers hesitated. And we took advantage of that.

"Ms. Light, the Guardian, Storm Lad: One by one the Rangers' ranks thinned as the Umbra Gun overtook them. With every blast one of them was wrapped in darkness and sucked into the Gloom. Eventually there were only a few of the heroes left—the Junior Rangers, who we never expected to be a problem. We were celebrating, all grouped around my father, the one firing the weapon. That's when Lone Star swooped in, his entire body burning so brightly that he looked like a falling meteor. The intensity in his face—the light pouring from his eyes . . ."

She trailed off, as if lost in the memory and unable to speak further.

"We never had a chance to fire. Lone Star landed in the middle of the group like a bomb, energy shooting off in every direction, scorching the ground and trees," Barrage said, picking up the story. "When the debris and dust cleared, the result of his attack was immediately evident. Lone Star stood in the center of a crater where Cloak had been a moment before. The four of us—your High Council—were all that survived."

"I was tapped into their minds," Shade said. "The final, anguished thoughts of all our fallen screamed in my head. What should have been our greatest triumph ended in the darkest day of Cloak's history."

Alex thought he could see tears forming in his mother's eyes, but he couldn't be sure. "We're going to avenge them," he said. "All of them. And we'll honor their memory when Justice Tower is in flames."

"We forget that you're young," Shade said, smiling softly first at Alex, then at the rest of the Betas. "You weren't there. How should we expect you to understand how much this attack means?"

"Of course we understand," Julie said. "We all lost something that day, even if we weren't old enough to remember it."

"We've been waiting for this all our lives," Titan said.

"It's all any of us want," Mallory agreed.

"It's our destiny," Alex said.

The council again looked at one another, nodding, as if they'd been waiting to hear such sentiments for a long time.

"Stay here," Shade said, rising from her seat. "I'll be right back."

She walked out into the hallway, leaving the others to

their dinner. Titan made small talk by boasting how much weight he'd added to his training regimen that week, and suggested that he use himself as a human wrecking ball during the attack. Alex was just beginning to say that he would happily use his powers to throw Titan through the walls when Shade returned, carrying four black boxes wrapped in gray ribbon.

"We were going to wait until the attack to give these to you," she said, passing the boxes out to the Betas. "But consider them rewards for completing your first mission."

The Betas opened the boxes and tore into the tissue paper. Alex's heart began to race as he realized what sat on the table in front of him. It was a lead-colored trench coat with a hood, lightweight and reinforced with thin bulletproof plates. On each shoulder were two silver bands.

Julie screamed and had her coat halfway on before any of the others even realized what they had been given.

"You're the future leaders of the Cloak Society," Phantom said. "You ought to look like it."

For a moment, everyone in the room beamed with joy.

"You should count yourselves lucky," Volt added. "When I was your age, we were still running around in heavy wool cloaks."

Shade stood and walked around the table to Alex. She pressed the lapels of the coat down, smoothed the shoulders out, and took a step back to get a better look at her son.

"My Alexander," Shade said, smiling. "How handsome you look in that."

She turned him around so that he could make himself out in the gleaming silver skull on the wall beside him. In its polished teeth, with his mother behind him, Alex cast an ominous reflection. His lips spread broadly across his face, but the metal distorted his smile.

8

POWER
TRAINING

Saturday.

Running. Breakfast. Tutoring. Lunch. Studying. Power training.

Alex rode the elevator to the surface in a black T-shirt and running shorts. He was looking forward to this power training session, and to showing his mother that he deserved the two silver bands on his new Cloak coat.

"Mother?" he called out as he stepped from the projection booth, expecting to see her waiting for him. "Hello?"

Since Shade's abilities gave her insight into the mind-set and limitations of her pupils, she handled power training, sometimes with assistance from Volt. Several times a week, the Betas met with her for one-on-one instruction.

Lessons varied, but the objectives were always the same: refinement, increased power, and control. Walking into a session with Shade, the Betas never had any idea as to what exactly they'd be doing. Mallory might be spending an hour attempting to freeze a single ice cube from across a room or creating smoldering infernos in an empty field. Julie's training often focused on hand-to-hand combat and agility, as well as attempting to spread her gemlike form to the rest of her body. This type of blind training had a purpose, according to Shade. After all, how could they ever truly know what to expect when walking into a potentially dangerous situation?

Alex walked around the abandoned drive-in parking lot, but his mother was nowhere to be found. Instead a square piece of paper was taped to one of the old speaker posts that dotted the lot. He recognized his mother's handwriting.

Alex,
Be right back. Start your warm-ups.

The breeze picked up, and the paper blew off the post, drifting away from Alex. He focused his mind on the page, stopping it in midair. His ears drew back slightly and the paper began to stir, folding in on itself. The movements were slow but precise, each edge crisp and evenly lined up. After a final tuck, a winged bird was floating in front of him.

He smiled to himself. Alex liked origami, the symmetry

of it, the thought that a piece of paper could be turned into something else with just a few creases and bends. When his mother first started training him, he was always tearing half-formed frogs or getting lost in the design. His mother had put emphasis on precision over power, stressing that mastering the former would lead to a better control of the latter. If nothing else, the accuracy of Alex's powers was improving. He had that to be proud of.

Alex willed the bird to flap its wings. It flew gracefully up into the air, until a popping sound came from somewhere in the trees lining the lot to Alex's right. A half second later, his paper bird was falling to the ground in pieces. Alex turned toward the direction the sound had come from but saw nothing in the dense screen of branches and trunks. Realizing that he was under attack, he ran toward the projection booth for cover.

Another *pop*, this time shooting dirt into the air just a few feet away from him. Something small and black bounced away from the point of impact. Alex pulled the black object to him with his thoughts. It was hot in his hands, a perfect sphere the size of a golf ball, firm but squishy, like an eraser.

"Mother . . . ," he muttered. He should have expected something like this. Leaving the safety of cover, he walked into the open, raising his arms into the sky. "You're shooting at me? Seriously?"

Alex's wits were about him now. The training session had

begun the moment he'd stepped off the elevator. Clever. His eyes scanned the trees for sight of his mother, but the cover was too good. Of course she wouldn't let him off that easily.

Pop. Another noise in front of him, slightly to the right. The ball whizzed by Alex's ear, close enough for him to feel its wake.

Pop. The next bullet was headed straight for his chest, but with a wave of his hand it was deflected off course. Two more shots immediately followed, but now that he knew where they were coming from, Alex stopped them easily. He flung them back toward the trees with a blue push.

More pops. Now another shooter had joined in the fray, firing just off to Alex's left. A ball grazed his left shoulder, stinging him. He was ready for the next shot, though, and as the two shooters pumped round after round toward Alex, he got into the rhythm of it and was sending the bullets back almost immediately after they were fired. *Hear the pop. See the ball. Focus. Push it back.*

As quickly as they'd begun, the shots stopped, and Alex stood panting in the center of the parking lot. Movement in the trees. Alex's parents emerged and walked toward him, carrying oversized black guns that were part rifle, part leaf blower. They were both dressed in dark T-shirts and pants with more pockets than anyone could possibly need.

"Nicely done, son," Volt said, once he was close enough that Alex could hear his voice.

"Remember to breathe," Shade added. "It doesn't matter how many bullets you deflect if you're just going to pass out."

"I feel good," Alex said, standing tall, anxious to show no weakness.

"Wonderful," Shade said, smiling. "That was just your warm-up. Come with me."

Shade led Alex to the back of the snack bar, where an old, padlocked wooden box sat on the ground. It was at least four feet long and stood several feet tall. Its hinges were rusty, and most of its white paint had weathered off long ago.

"Inside this box is a generator that weighs just over five hundred pounds," Shade said, walking around the perimeter of the container. "I want you to lift the box and its contents off the ground."

"That's impossible," Alex said. He looked to his father, his eyes urging the man to protest along with him. "There is no way I can pick that up."

"Just try, son," Volt said. "That's all we're asking you to do."

"I'm telling you, I can't do it," Alex said. "Let me start with something smaller. I can work my way up."

"We've *been* doing smaller things," Shade said. "Tables. Chairs. Just a few days ago you tossed a girl several yards with only the slightest effort."

"Fine," Alex said. The last thing he wanted was to talk

about Kirbie again. He narrowed his eyes and focused, placing his hands in front of him, palms wide.

"Hands down, Alex," his mother said. "Flexing your arms is just wasting energy."

Alex pressed his lips together and set his jaw. Breathing in a few deep gulps of air, he lowered his arms and focused his mind on the box in front of him. Everything around it faded away as the box glowed blue. Alex lifted, straining his brain until it felt like fire would shoot from his head. The lock on the front of the box jiggled.

"Harder," Shade said from Alex's left.

This was just like the vault, he thought. His palms went clammy down at his sides. *Do it,* he pleaded silently. *Rise. Rise off the ground. Just a little. Please.*

The dirt around the box shifted. The breeze seemed to change.

"That's it," Shade cooed in a reassuring manner.

Eyes bulging, muscles tense, Alex pushed at the box.

And then, nothing. Alex exhaled loudly and shook his head as if he were coming out of a trance. When his eyes met his mother's, she was frowning.

"I see we'll have to do this another way," Shade said calmly.

She led him back to the drive-in parking lot. As they walked, Volt took a small electronic device out of his pocket and began tapping on it.

"Stand there," Shade said, pointing to a clear area in the center of the lot. "Tell me: How did you go about stopping those bullets earlier?"

"What do you mean?" Alex asked.

"Walk us through it," she said.

"Well . . ." Alex paused. He was never very good at describing how it was he saw the world. "I could see the bullets coming toward me, so I focused on each one . . . and they would start to shine. Blue, like everything else. And when that happened, it's like I could *feel* the bullet. I just stopped it and pushed it back toward you. Once I got the hang of it, it was easy."

"You performed very well—even if you were caught off guard at first," his mother said, a small smile forming on her lips.

"We're ready," Volt said, looking up from his electronic device.

"Wonderful. Look around you, Alex," his mother said, motioning widely with one arm. "What do you see on the roof over there?"

A weapon similar to the ones Shade and Volt were carrying appeared over the snack bar, rising from behind the lip of the roof. It twisted, shifting its aim until it pointed directly at Alex. Another appeared, perched on the edge of the movie screen. Alex saw it calibrating out of the corner of his eye.

"Uh . . . ," he murmured.

"There are five guns currently trained on you," Shade stated casually. "On my signal, they will go off at the same time, and will fire with increasing strength until I tell them to quit."

"But it would be impossible for me to stop all of those," Alex said, his voice soft.

"The way you stopped the others, yes," she said. "There's no way you could stop each bullet individually."

"You're going to *shoot* me."

"Only if you don't think of another way to stop them. They're only rubber bullets shot at a controlled velocity," Volt said. "They're not lethal."

"Yeah, but they hurt!" Alex said. "I don't want to do this!"

"You don't have a choice," Shade snapped, her calm demeanor breaking. "It's your duty to hone your skills for the good of us all, and if this is how it must be done, then so be it."

"But Mother—"

"I am not your mother right now," she replied. "I am the person in charge of making sure you use your powers to the best of your ability. If you can't do that, then you are a liability, and Cloak has no use for you."

"Alex," Volt said. "The only way Cloak succeeds is if we are all performing at our highest capabilities. You know this. One day you will thank us for today. Trust me. It's for your own good."

"Your telekinesis—this blue energy—is all around you," Shade said. "It's in the air. It *is* the air. You tend to associate it with objects. The bullets, for instance. Or the paper. But the energy comes from *you* and it's yours to manipulate. So create a shield. A force-field bubble to protect you. It's the only way you'll make it out of this exercise without getting hurt."

"Fine," Alex said. Paper birds and unmoved boxes weren't going to impress them. "Let's do this."

His mother and father smiled and backed away.

"I'll give you four counts, and then we fire," Shade said. "Make me proud."

Alex looked up at her, exhaled a long breath, and nodded.

"Four."

Alex closed his eyes. He reached out with his mind, imagining the energy rising, folding and collecting itself like a blue origami shell. He pushed at it with his thoughts, forming a protective layer.

"Three."

Alex could sense that the force field was too thin. He gritted his teeth and poured more energy into the bubble.

"Two."

The telekinetic power was pouring out of him now. The walls were strengthening. Alex opened his eyes and saw the brilliant blue light of the bubble, glimmering as if it were real.

"One."

The popping was instantaneous, coming from all sides. Alex braced for impact, clenching every muscle in his body.

But the impact never came. Instead the bullets bounced off his makeshift shield. The guns continued firing—Alex could feel thuds growing more violent with every round—but his force field held. There was a satisfied expression on his mother's face, a look of pride that he so rarely saw in her eyes.

"Yes!" she yelled at him. "Good! Keep going!"

It was an awful test. Alex wanted nothing more than to impress his parents and to be back on the strike team, but this was bordering on torture. He knew it was for the glory of Cloak, but he was sure that kids weren't supposed to be shot at by their parents. The guns continued to fire, and with each round Alex grew more upset. His anger pushed out of him and into the bubble, feeding it. The force field began to expand, and the earth flattened around Alex in a perfect circle, growing steadily outward.

"Alex, that's enough," Shade said, but the circle grew, encroaching on them steadily. "Volt is stopping the guns. There will be no more bullets. I promise."

But Alex wasn't listening. He was so focused on the force field that he didn't even notice the shots had stopped coming.

"Alexander!" Shade yelled again, but still, he didn't respond. She tried to reach out with her mind, but her thoughts bounced off the invisible energy, and the resulting backlash made her head ring.

The situation had suddenly become dangerous. She nodded to Volt, who threw his arm forward, sending an arching spray of purple electricity toward his son. When it hit the edge of the invisible dome, it bounced off, hitting one of the rusted speaker boxes, which then erupted in a shower of sparks.

"ALEXANDER!" Shade shouted.

As the bubble pressed up against the speaker boxes, the posts holding them up snapped like they were made of Styrofoam. Shade focused and gritted her teeth, ignoring the throbbing in her head as she tried to force her thoughts through her son's defenses. Her silver eyes were radiant in the sun as she finally broke into Alex's mind.

STOP! she screamed in his head with all her power. *NOW!*

His mother's mental intrusion startled him, and what little control Alex had over the bubble was wiped away. It expanded wildly, and for the first time Shade and Volt could see it—the crackling blue energy their son always spoke of, brilliant and untamed. The bubble passed over Shade and Volt as it grew, sending them sprawling backward. A cloud of reddish dirt rose from the wake of the force. Finally the shield dissipated, until it was nothing more than a counter-current against the breeze.

"Are you all right?" Volt asked his wife as he sat up. She nodded, coughing, and waved toward their son, who was on his knees. Volt was on his feet in a flash.

"I did it, right?" Alex asked as his father crouched beside him.

"Yes, you did," Volt said as he took Alex's face in one hand, turning it from side to side in inspection. "But it looks like you have a bit of a nosebleed."

"Here," Shade said, standing. She patted at her legs. "I have a bandage in one of these pockets."

She finally came across a short length of gauze and balled it up. She knelt beside Alex and pressed the cloth to his nose, letting her free hand rub his back.

"I'd say that's enough for the day," Volt said. "You did a great job, son."

"Aren't you going to show him?" Shade asked. "That *was* the point of all this."

"The boy has been through a lot, dear," Volt said. Shade's face grew sour, staring back at him.

"Show me what?" Alex asked.

Shade helped her son to his feet. He was wobbly at first,

but was able to stand and walk without the support of his parents. She led him to the back of the snack bar once again, where she stopped before the box.

"I can't do anything else today . . . ," Alex started. As he spoke, Shade produced a key from one of her pockets and removed the container's lock.

"Open it," she said.

Hesitantly Alex bent down and lifted the lid. The rusted hinges creaked. Inside, the box was empty except for a few handfuls of gravel.

"Where's the generator?" Alex asked, confused.

"Titan moved it," Shade said flatly. "It was part of his training a few days ago. This box you couldn't lift weighed twenty pounds, at most."

"That doesn't make any sense," Alex said, still trying to wrap his mind around what he was seeing. "I tried as hard as I could."

"And you couldn't do it," his mother said. "But when you were in danger just now, you displayed incredible power. You were acting on instinct to save yourself. That's what we have to fix. You need to channel that power into something you can control at will. What were you feeling when you created that force field?"

"I just didn't want to get hurt."

"And?" Shade asked.

"Fear," Alex said after a pause. "And anger."

"Good," Shade said. "It's not your thoughts that fuel your telekinesis, Alex. It's your feelings. You have to learn to use that anger—that hatred—against your enemies."

"And you had to shoot at me and lie to me to prove this point," Alex said, his hands curling into fists at his sides. If anger was truly what fueled his powers, he felt as if he could flatten the entire drive-in at that moment.

"You are the only thing keeping you from reaching your full potential, Alex," Shade said. "We had to show you."

"Are we done with this session?" Alex asked. "I think I'd like to go inside."

"Of course," his mother replied.

Alex walked toward the elevator, his muscles knotted and sore. He trembled from the combination of stress and anger and exertion.

"Alex," his mother called to him before he rounded the corner of the snack bar.

He turned to see her standing close to his father, her right hand raised up beside her face.

"For the glory," she said.

Alex stared back at her, then turned away.

9

THE
GLOOM

Alex woke with a start. He hadn't meant to fall asleep, but the training exercise had been so strenuous that he'd passed out as soon as he got back to his room. Rolling over, blinking, he looked at the space where his alarm clock usually sat before remembering the accident earlier in the week. Attempting to shake off his sleepiness, he crept over to his desk and picked up his wristwatch. It was a few minutes after eleven p.m. He'd just taken a six-hour nap.

Wonderful, he thought. *Now I'm going to be up all night.*

Alex sat down in his desk chair and spun around a few times, taking an inventory of his room, wondering what he should do. Thoughts of the afternoon rushed to his head. The more he tried to ignore them, the stronger they became. That embarrassing empty box. The rubber bullets. His anger at his mother and father. And at the same time, all the shame and regret he had in connection to Kirbie—for saving her, and for failing to do anything about their accidental meeting—pitted themselves in his stomach.

Potential. It was a word his parents often used when talking about him. They had never tried to hide their hope that he would grow to be the most powerful member of Cloak, and while this had thrilled Alex, he had never really believed it possible. How could he hope to fare against a behemoth like Titan, whose powers were such that he was always Titan? Now Alex *had* exhibited impressive strength, but it had served only to confuse him. How was he supposed to deal with a problem that was in his head?

Shuffling through some papers on his desk, he found the photograph his father had given him the day after his birthday. With all the excitement about the news broadcast that night, he had forgotten all about it.

Alex scrounged for a thumbtack and pinned the photo up on his wall with his other pictures and news clippings. He stepped back, staring at the photo of his grandfather, the man who had died for Cloak and therefore for Alex. Perhaps if his grandfather were still around, he could teach Alex the secret to living up to his full potential and making his parents smile like they had in the photograph. After all, he was the man who'd led the charge at Victory Park, the one responsible for banishing all those Rangers to the Gloom. If anyone represented all that the Cloak Society stood for, surely it was him.

What could he do to prove himself worthy of being his grandfather's descendant?

Proof, Alex thought. *That's all I need.*

He wanted to get out of his room for a bit and clear his head. If he was lucky, Gage was still awake and tinkering around his workshop. Maybe his friend would sneak him to the surface for a while, or at least brainstorm ways to help get him back on the attack team. It was late, and Alex walked lightly in the hallway, his footsteps padding on the cement, and called the elevator.

Unfortunately, Gage wasn't in his workshop, but Alex decided to wait for him. He walked around, running his fingers over a few objects scattered on Gage's worktables, wondering what they might do. He picked a laser rifle up off a counter and peered through its scope. Apart from his mother, Cloak members rarely used such things, but Alex was well trained with them nonetheless, and the base was stocked full of all kinds of weapons so that in the unlikely event of an attack, the Unibands could take up arms. As he held the rifle, he imagined scores of loyal soldiers following him into battle, brandishing Cloak weaponry. Maybe when they took Sterling City, he could set up his own security detail—his own personal fleet of knights.

Alex's arm caught a metal rod hanging off a counter, sending a shower of screws and wires and a small metal cube falling to the floor. A light on one of the box's sides began to blink, accompanied by a quiet hum. After a few seconds, the light faded, as did the noise, but Alex remained frozen until he was sure he hadn't accidentally activated some sort of miniature bomb. Carefully he picked the objects up off the floor and set down the rifle. His heart racing, he made his way to the center workspace, keeping his fingers tucked in at his sides as he progressed.

Blueprints, sketches, and notes were spread about the table. Alex recognized Gage's handwriting on them. Alex had no idea what the notes meant—he wasn't sure half the words were English—but the drawings and blueprints were easier to understand. As he flipped through a worn notebook, he saw page after page of sketches showing modifications of the same weapon, with notes jotted hastily off to the side of each one.

It wasn't like Gage to go through so many drafts of a single item. Usually he just sat thinking about a design for as long as necessary and then produced a single, final schematic.

Underneath the notebook was a piece of yellowing paper covered with a different handwriting, not unlike Gage's. A single word jumped off the page at Alex: Umbra. He was looking at one of the few notes Gage's father had left about the weapon. A chill of excitement raced down Alex's spine.

The drawing only served to remind him of the impending mission. And once more, his mind was flooded with every mistake he'd made in the past week. The vault door. The empty box. Kirbie.

It was then that Alex realized there was a simple solution to all his problems. Kirbie had been at the root of it all, had been the reason he was suspended to begin with. And he knew where she was. Alone—on night duty at Victory Park. Not only that, he had told her such an exquisite lie that he could easily catch her off guard. To her, he was a possible ally. He could exploit her weakness and capture her. What better way to prove that he was worthy of being a member of Cloak than by presenting the girl who had caused him so much trouble to the High Council?

Excitement surged through him. Around him, he could feel the air crackle and pop with blue light. The only problem was how to get to the park. He could maybe get Gage to send him aboveground through the elevator, but he'd still be miles and miles away from his destination. He needed something quick. Something clandestine.

The safe house. It was located close to the eastern edge of Victory Park, hidden in an inconspicuous office building, and served as their rendezvous point if a mission ever went sour or an emergency befell a Cloak member within the city. But more importantly, there was a way to travel between the safe house and the underground base without setting off any alarms.

His eyes fell on the Gassers and Blackout Bombs that Gage had shown him. He called one of each with his thoughts and placed them in separate back pockets. He could use the Gasser to take Kirbie down, and the Blackout Bomb if he needed a quick cover beneath the streetlights. The safe house was close enough to Victory Park that he could conceivably float her back without running into anyone on the street. Blending into darkness and evading detection were two of the first skills perfected by members of Cloak, after all. And if he did meet with trouble, well, he was a member of the most powerful secret society in the world—it wouldn't be a problem. All he had to do was take the initiative.

Before he could talk himself out of it, Alex went briskly to the exit.

He peeked outside and, seeing no one, walked farther down the wing to an unmarked door at the end of the hall. Beside it a rectangular electronic screen was mounted on the wall. He held his right hand up to the screen and pressed his palm against it. The mark of Cloak tingled in response, cold, bubbling to the surface. The screen flashed for a moment, and then the door slid open.

He stared into the blackness before him, knowing not

to bother searching for a light switch. As he stepped inside, the door closed behind him as a dim bulb flickered on above him, lighting the room only enough for him to make out the steel walls and concrete floor. It was hardly bigger than a broom closet. The only thing of note was a square inset in the wall across from the entrance, which seemed to gleam with an eerie light of its own. Alex's hand tingled, as if the box in the wall was calling to him. The black skull and hood surfaced again on the palm of his hand.

Alex was looking at one of Gage's father's greatest inventions: a transportation device that utilized Phantom's dark energy and mimicked the workings of her power—a byproduct of his work on the Umbra Gun. The transporter was generally used for emergency purposes only, but also served as a discreet way for people like Misty's mother to visit the compound.

Alex stood for a moment, telling himself that traveling through the Gloom was a small price to pay for the chance to be back on the team. He could feel the box pulling at his palm with some invisible force, like a powerful magnet, calling him to step forward. Slowly he moved his hand toward the black recess. The force grew, until Alex wasn't sure that he could jerk away even if he wanted to. The darkness embedded in his palm grew over the back of his hand as it entered the box. Black energy expanded until it covered his wrist, shimmering like ink as it began to snake its way up his arm. It traveled up to his shoulder and across his chest, sending chills all over his body. Within a few seconds he was almost entirely covered. He took a deep breath and closed his eyes as the energy moved over his face and head. Before he could give it a second thought, he was sucked into the Gloom.

The weightlessness and freezing, right down to his core, were the same as they had been in the Gloom just days before. But the rate at which Alex floated through the plane was slower without Phantom pulling him along. The wind passed like a strong breeze instead of a tempest, allowing him to breathe normally. The air was thin and cold, stinging his nostrils. His right palm was outstretched, and he could feel it being guided across the barren place to the other side of Sterling City.

Again, the sounds of moaning—of anguish—drifted through the air. Alex told himself it was just the wind and his overactive imagination. Against his better judgment, he opened his eyes, wondering if he could get an idea of how close he was to the safe house. Faint light filtered in from overhead, and Alex's eyes adjusted to the Gloom. Suddenly he was getting his first real look at the hidden realm. Where before he could make out only swirls of darkness, he now saw distinct shapes. Structures that looked like they were built solely from shadows lay in ruins, as if at some point civilization had actually existed there and people had constructed shelters from its ruins. And there were other things, too: stones and bricks and plants that looked like they had come from Alex's world and been left there. He wondered if this was Phantom's doing. If the Gloom was a land over which she could truly be queen, she might have built a kingdom for herself over the years.

As he traveled, the sounds of howling and yelling became louder, until it was impossible for Alex to tell himself that it was just the wind. Something was alive in the Gloom. With every passing second the volume grew louder, terrifying Alex, who looked around frantically for the source of the cries. There were nothing but shadows and half-formed hovels barely standing out against the pools of darkness that made up the landscape.

Then, out of the corner of his eye, he saw movement. Something was walking out of the blackness. Squinting, he could make out a wan figure in the distance. Its face was gaunt and skeletal with sunken, lifeless eyes. It opened its mouth, and the same howling noise he'd heard on the way back from the bank mission pounded on his eardrums. Alex couldn't look away—could barely breathe—as he came to the terrifying realization that this was probably someone from his world stranded there by Phantom. Alex couldn't help but wonder if he was looking at one of the Rangers of Justice who had been beaten in Victory Park ten years before, left to wander the Gloom endlessly. He'd been celebrating the Umbra Gun for the past week but had never stopped to think what it meant to be banished into such a purgatory, doomed to wander undying. And for how long? Forever? No one knew.

Alex couldn't stand it any longer. He closed his eyes and covered his ears and wished the horrible vision away.

10

FULL
COLOR

When Alex opened his eyes again, he was in a small room almost identical to the one in the underground base. The overhead lights burned dimly. He trembled, horrified by what he'd just seen, and hurried over to the electronic screen on the wall, shoving his palm against it. All he wanted to do was get far away from the Gloom. After a flash, the wall before him shifted and a panel slid aside.

He stumbled into the new room. The transporter was hidden in the back of a long closet, where he now stood, flanked on both sides by dark-colored clothing. Alex hurried through, his hands pushing over the hanging shirts and pants and jackets, sending several of them falling to the floor. Then he headed through the master bedroom, furnished only with a bed and dresser, and into the rest of the apartment. He collapsed on a sofa—one of the few objects in the sparsely decorated living area—and tried to calm down. Cloak members of all rank and order traveled the Gloom on a daily basis, he told himself. So what if the Rangers of Justice were slowly rotting away there? They were his enemies. It was okay. Everything would be okay.

Despite these thoughts, Alex couldn't calm down. He needed to be outside, where there was fresh air and open space and the shadows didn't move on their own. The safe house was located in the basement of a building owned by a subsidiary of Cloak, and the building manager and staff were all paid enough to turn a blind eye to the "storage space" secured behind an electronic lock. Alex found another blank screen beside a door in the living room and waved his palm in front of it. With a loud click, the thick metal door moved toward him an inch, and he pulled it open to reveal the dank cement floor of the building's basement. Alex pulled the door shut behind him and made his way up the stairs to his right, which led to the street. There was a wrought-iron gate blocking his way, but with a little con-centration, he felt out the innards of the simple locking mechanism, and one metallic click later, he was standing on the sidewalk of downtown Sterling City.

Alex gasped for air, his body feeling light from the relief of being outdoors. He stared up happily at the full moon, surrounded by thick clouds. Adrenaline pumped through his veins. The city at night—at least this part of it—was practically monochromatic, all varying shades of gray brick giving way to sidewalk and asphalt. The office building sat in the middle of a narrow, one-way block, lit only by the streetlamps that dotted the sidewalk infrequently. Alex could see why this location had been chosen. The street was quiet and offered large patches of darkness in which to hide.

He pushed all thoughts of the Gloom out of his mind and stepped into the street, getting his bearings, rehearsing what he might say to Kirbie while he waited for the perfect moment to hit her with the Gasser. In the distance, he could see Justice Tower rising out of the cultural district just north of Victory Park. The opaque dome on its top blazed, piercing the sky with a shaft of light.

He kept his guard up and head down as he walked the few blocks to the park, though he passed no one. The financial district was quiet this time of night, but Alex was ready to slip into an alley at the first sign of trouble. A block from the park, he passed a building facade under construction and fenced in by tall panels of plywood. Pasted up on these boards were oversized posters, each featuring an adult member of the Rangers of Justice, chins held high, gazing triumphantly into the distance. At the bottom of each was a single word, printed in red, white, or blue. JUSTICE. TRUTH. PEACE. Alex glanced around, then ripped them all down with a single sharp thought.

Victory Park sat quiet, dark for the most part and closed for the night. He knew that most people thought the park was dangerous after sunset, swarming with ruffians and modern bandits of all sorts, but to Alex it looked inviting—common muggers and thieves had more to fear from him, after all.

Though he'd studied maps and knew the layout fairly well, Alex had never actually set foot in Victory Park before. He'd seen much of Sterling City on his Thursday afternoons or the other rare occasions that his parents took him out, but all requests to spend an afternoon in the park had been denied. The council had no desire to parade the Betas around the site of their greatest defeat. The place was a mess of paths and small roads intertwining throughout five hundred acres, and Alex chose one that seemed to run alongside Victory Circle, the street that bordered the park. The gravel beneath his feet gave a satisfying crunch to his footfalls, and he walked slowly, savoring his time, wondering if he should cause some sort of commotion to signal to Kirbie that he was there. Would she be in her wolf form, stalking through the trees? No, he thought. Tactically she'd do better as a bird, flying overhead with keen eyes.

Alex tilted his head back, staring up at the patchwork pieces of sky visible through the canopy of trees. The moon was positioned perfectly, full and luminous directly above him. Thick gray clouds were rolling across the sky, cutting the night light in and out like a slowly blinking strobe light. Focused on the sky, he didn't notice that the path was curving inward, moving farther away from the street and his only real point of geographical reference. Victory Park had swallowed him completely.

A faint shadow flew over the path ahead of him, breaking the calm moonlight. It was too fast to be a cloud. Too small. Alex looked up but saw nothing.

The path he'd chosen was winding and twisted every few yards. For all Alex knew, he might have been charging straight into Victory Circle with every turn. Eventually he spotted a glowing orb in the distance. Alex walked toward it until he recognized where he was from photographs and maps he'd studied. He was in the dead center of Victory Park, and before him, Centennial Fountain was radiant. A handful of wealthy citizens had donated an absurd amount of money to commission a sculpture for the town's one-hundredth anniversary not too long ago. The result was a bronze sculpture of the legendary Gordian knot, all twisted metal ropes wrapped around a blazing light, water gushing out of the center. Alex found it stunning.

"You came," a voice said from behind him.

Surprised, Alex sprung around, instinctively taking a defensive position. Kirbie stood in her Rangers uniform. She raised her arms in front of her, ready to fight him if necessary, though her expression was one of concern and not aggression.

"Jeez," Alex said, relaxing a bit. "You scared the crap out of me."

"Oh, sorry," Kirbie said cautiously. "I didn't realize you were so caught up in the fountain. It's really beautiful at night."

"Yeah," Alex said. "It is."

They were both unsure of how to proceed. Alex had his hands at his sides, his thumb grazing the outlines of the Gasser in his back pocket.

"If this is some sort of trap, I know this park like the back of my hand, and I've got a communicator with me," Kirbie said. "I can call for backup in half a second."

"Calm down. I just wanted to talk," Alex lied. "You *did* say that would be okay."

He shrugged, trying to look as innocent as possible. Kirbie sighed, raising a hand to her head.

"I'm sorry," she said. "You're right."

As she spoke, Alex concentrated on the Gasser, willing it to float out of his pocket and into the air, where he kept it hidden behind his back.

"It's just been a really weird week," Kirbie continued. "First with the bank and then at the mall. I mean, you're supposed to be my enemy, but you keep popping up and helping me out. I don't think I'd be standing here if it weren't for you. I guess what I'm trying to say is . . ."

"Uh-huh?" Alex murmured. Kirbie's focus was on the

ground. She was caught up in her words. It was now or never.

"Thank you," Kirbie said, letting her eyes meet his. "Thank you for saving my life."

Suddenly several strange things happened at once, none of which Alex fully understood. His head felt light and clear. The hairs on the back of his neck stood on end, and there was a feeling in his chest that he had never experienced before, one that bordered both pride and accomplishment. But most puzzling of all, Alex could *see* Kirbie—not bathed in blue like everything else in his world, but in full color.

Her blond hair gleamed. Her lips were a soft pink. Even in the dim lighting of the fountain, he could make out her hazel eyes. Alex didn't move—didn't breathe—just stood there staring at her, drinking in the colors, feeling happy, for the first time in recent memory. The sight of her was completely disarming.

He blinked, and Kirbie was once more tinted a cobalt blue. Alex's head ached, as if two waves had just crashed against each other in his brain. His focus on the device floating behind him faltered, and the Gasser flew backward, plopping into the fountain. He staggered back a few steps.

"Oh, hey," Kirbie said, stepping toward him. "Are you okay? You look really pale. Maybe you should sit down."

"What was that?" he muttered to himself as he made his way to the edge of the fountain and sat.

"What was what?" Kirbie asked. "I was just thanking

you, and you act as if you were shot or something."

"I'm sorry," he said, "I just . . . I felt dizzy for a second."

Why—how—had he just seen Kirbie in color? When his powers had first manifested, his mother had assured him that one day, when he was fully in control, he'd be able to see things clearly once again. But that was just speculation, and this had felt like quite the opposite of control.

"Are you sure you're okay?" Kirbie asked. "I can take you to the hospital or something. It's not far away."

"No, no," he said quickly. "Don't worry about it. I'm already feeling better."

Kirbie bit her lip, unsure what else to do.

"What's your name?" she asked.

"Alex."

"No, I mean your code name," she said. "Shouldn't it be, like, Dark Thought or something? I think that blond kid called himself 'Titan' about a million times while we were fighting."

"Yeah . . . that sounds like him," Alex said. "He's an idiot."

"I kind of gathered that."

Alex chuckled, then, realizing what he was doing, stopped immediately. His mind raced as he fought to remind himself why he was there in the first place. But things hadn't gone as he'd planned. The Gasser was drenched, surely worthless. What was he supposed to do now? If he attacked her and lost, he'd be thrown in jail. Better to continue talking, he thought. Besides, this was perhaps the first real conversation he had ever had with someone outside of the Cloak Society. Despite everything he was raised to think, Alex found himself anxious to hear what else she thought of the Beta Team and Cloak.

"I'm not really into the whole code-name thing," he said finally. "Plus, my last name is Knight, which is kind of cool enough already."

"Night. Darkness. Shadows. Sounds about right for someone in Cloak."

"No, it's Knight with a *K*," he said. "Like chivalry and King Arthur and all that."

Chivalry? King Arthur? What was he talking about? He felt more and more like Misty as the words tumbled from his mouth.

"You're Kirbie, right?" he asked, even though he knew the answer.

"Yeah. That's me."

"Just Kirbie? Aren't the other Junior Rangers called Thorn and Amp? Don't try to tell me those aren't code names too."

"Just Kirbie," she said. "My brother keeps calling me 'Fauna,' but I'm holding out for something better."

"Animal Girl has a nice ring to it," he said, grinning in spite of himself.

"I'm going to pretend you didn't say that."

"So that guy *is* your brother," Alex said.

"Kyle. Thorn. Yeah, we're twins."

"And he, what . . . controls plants, right?" Alex asked. He could use this information to help flesh out Cloak's profiles on the Junior Rangers.

"Yeah." Kirbie nodded. "He can make them grow or shrink and move around at will. He's kind of incredible."

"The Nature Twins," Alex said.

"I'm going to have to arrest you," she said flatly.

Alex tensed up, but Kirbie smiled, and he realized she was kidding.

"So you're really going to defect from Cloak?" she asked.

"Well . . . ," Alex started, choosing his words carefully, "I want to. But I just don't know that I can. It's complicated."

"Why did you push me out of the way when Titan threw that hydrant at me?" she asked. "Surely that didn't go over well with everyone else."

"No. Not at all. I'm in big trouble now, actually. But it didn't seem right, you getting hurt like that," Alex said, feeling a little relieved to admit this to someone who he knew would agree with him. "I mean, Titan was so gung ho about defeating you that I figured he wasn't pulling any punches, so . . ."

"Of course not," she said. "He's a criminal. The Cloak

154

Society are supervillains. Killing is kind of what they do, isn't it?"

"Sort of, but . . ." Alex was having trouble putting into words what he hadn't dared think about since the mission. But there beneath the light of Centennial Fountain it all came pouring out. "Before now it's all been imaginary. Like a game. The missions and planning and everything were just things we talked about hypothetically. I know in the end everything will be worth it, and I want to live up to what my parents expect of me . . . but I don't think I have it in me to kill somebody. Even if they are my enemy."

Kirbie stared at him, doubtful.

"Then don't," she said.

Alex opened his mouth to protest this, but found that he didn't know what to say.

Suddenly Kirbie jumped to her feet and stared intently at something in the distance. Her face contorted, but Alex saw nothing but sky, towering buildings, and the reflections of streetlights in mirrored windows. Then he realized that one of the lights was moving in their direction, in front of the clouds, and growing larger by the second.

"What is that?" Alex asked, standing.

"Lux. My mentor. One of the Rangers. She's team leader tonight, patrolling downtown. She'll be coming to check on me."

She turned and looked at Alex. Her eyes were earnest.

"Do you want to come with me? Back to Justice Tower?"

Alex stared, dumbfounded by this suggestion. For a half second, he considered it. But despite what he had said to Kirbie, he was and always would be a member of the Cloak Society. It was in his blood. It was written on his palm.

"No," Alex asked. "I can't."

"Fine," she said, visibly disappointed. "But you have to get out of here. If Lux finds out I've been talking to you without telling anyone, I'll be in huge trouble."

She turned away from him, taking a crouched stance, ready to soar into the night air.

"Can I see you again?" he asked.

She turned and stared at him, trying to make sense of his expression. Alex's eyes fell to the ground. The words had surprised him as much as they had her.

"I mean, if you're around," Alex continued. "If you're watching the park. Will I run into you again?"

"I'll be here again next weekend," she said.

"Okay," Alex said.

Kirbie smiled fully for the first time that evening. "Think about what I said. It's your life, Alex. Not Cloak's."

Alex nodded slowly. "Have a good night," he said, and backed away, into the comfortable shadows of the surrounding trees. He watched as an oversized golden bird soared into the air, flying straight for the glowing figure in the distance. Squinting, he could just make out the form of a woman in the light, her hair luminescent. Kirbie circled her, flying with exquisite grace, before continuing off in the direction opposite of where Alex was. The glowing woman followed, and Alex watched as they alighted on a rooftop on the other side of the park, tiny specks against the sky.

Alex's mind was a jumble as he made his way back to the street. He should have felt unhappy, shamed by yet another failure on his part. But he didn't. In fact, he felt better about himself than he had all day. His mind wandered to Gage's earlier caution not to sympathize with the enemy, but he shook this warning away. He and Kirbie had only been talking. There was no harm in that.

The path eventually led him to the street, but not his original entrance. Instead he stood across from Silver Bank, towering and living up to its name in the moonlight. Alex stared at it for a moment. Then he sprinted across the street and turned, heading toward the safe house, leaving the bank behind him.

Traveling through the Gloom back to his home, he kept his eyes clamped shut and hands over his ears. He had no desire to see what was lurking in that place. He thought only of the golden-haired girl, and the colors and lightness she had brought to him. Of the Gloom, he preferred to be ignorant.

11

CAPTURE
THE FLAG

The following morning, Alex lay on top of his bed in confusion. Kirbie was the enemy. They were archrivals, destined to hate each other. And yet, talking with her last night had seemed like the most natural thing in the world. She wanted to help him. Was this what the Rangers of Justice were about? And if he was falling for it, did that mean Alex was weak-minded, like the citizens of Sterling City? As he mulled over these questions, his mind kept returning to the skeletal figure in the Gloom. He hated to admit it, but part of him didn't want to see Kirbie banished to that place. Luckily, the attack on Justice Tower was still months away. His focus had to be getting back on that team. Kirbie would be back at Victory Park next weekend, and he could still turn her over to the High Council. Who knew—maybe with their help, she would defect to their side. He would like that.

He had just finished brushing his teeth when a knock came at the door. Expecting a wake-up call from Mallory, he walked over to the entryway. But to his surprise, Shade stood in the hallway, looking a bit tired but composed in the long black trench usually reserved for missions. A cup of coffee in a blue mug was in her hand. The sharp smell of dark-roast beans filled Alex's nostrils.

"Good morning, son," Shade said before blowing across the top of her cup. "How did you sleep?"

"Oh, Mother," Alex said. "Um, great. I slept great."

They stood there for a moment, the steam of the coffee rising into the air between them. *She knows,* he thought. *She knows everything.* Alex's mind raced, building up a mental block and hiding all thoughts and memories of the previous night.

"Well, aren't you going to invite your mother in?" she finally asked.

"Of course, yeah. Come on in."

It was rare that his mother stopped by for a visit. Normally, if she needed to speak with him, she'd simply let her voice ring in his head or send a message with someone else. Alex expected that there was some sort of lecture coming.

"I want to talk to you about yesterday," she started.

"What about it?" Alex asked tentatively.

"About your training. About the way it was handled."

"Oh." Alex exhaled.

Shade walked around her son's room. To Alex's relief, she didn't seem to notice the piles of dirty clothes on the floor, or general messiness of the room. Instead she stopped in front of the wall where his newspaper clippings and photos were taped. She recognized a few of the headlines. SUPER-POWERED GROUP INVADES MUSEUM GALA. MISSING ART LINKED TO SECRET SOCIETY. MYSTERIOUS 'CLOAK SOCIETY': FACT OR FICTION? With her right hand she reached out, tracing the edges of the yellowing paper, until her finger fell on the photo of Alex's grandfather—her father—on the wall.

"You know, when I was your age, there was really no one around to teach us how to use our powers. Back then Cloak was different. They were unified, but they weren't serious. The Society was more like a country club for people with superpowers than the force it should have been. Our founders were people of determination, and of course they had goals, but my father's High Council seemed happy to forever operate from the shadows. My generation wanted more. We wanted to push ourselves as far as we could, to show the world that we were its zenith. And it cost us almost everything. After Victory Park, I swore that I would never again let someone from Cloak fall because we weren't prepared."

"But what happened at Victory Park wasn't anyone's

fault," Alex interjected. "Who could have known that Lone Star was so powerful?"

Shade nodded slightly, sipping from her coffee cup.

"Be that as it may, we should never have needed the Umbra Gun to begin with," she said. "There were so many of us then, with such extraordinary gifts. But we were undisciplined, unprepared. No one had the control over their powers that they should have.

"You may think that your father and I are pushing you too hard, but it is only because we know that you are going to do great things. Even just yesterday, you showed huge progress. You will help bring Cloak into a golden age, Alex. You want that, don't you? To make us proud?"

"Of course," he said. "More than anything."

Shade moved to him, tousling his hair.

"My Alexander. You will be Cloak's ultimate weapon. Our sword. Titan may be strong, but he is nothing compared to what you will be. People will tremble before you. The country will whisper your name with fear and reverence. When we're done with your training, you will be the greatest power this world has ever known."

She looked into his eyes.

"I apologize for lying to you about the box, but everything I do, everything any of us do, is for the good of Cloak. And what is good for Cloak is good for you. Do you understand?"

Alex stared back at her and nodded.

"Now, get your training uniform on. We're doing a group exercise in the field today, and you're expected up top soon. You can thank me later for the way I've split the teams," she said, opening the door and stepping into the hallway. "Make me proud, son."

She glanced back at him.

"And clean this room up. It's disgusting."

The door shut, leaving Alex alone once again. His heart thumped in his chest. She had apologized—a marvel in itself. But more importantly, she had reminded him that the confusion of his morning was completely uncalled-for. He had a destiny. He would rise to be Cloak's greatest asset. There was no room for thoughts of Kirbie or the fate of the Rangers in his mind.

Turning to his closet, he found himself greeted by his uniform, still folded, floating in front of him. Blue energy crackled around it. But he hadn't been consciously focused on his uniform, only thinking of it somewhere in the back of his mind. His subconscious must have summoned the clothes—something he didn't even know was possible.

He plucked them from the air, staring at them in mild concern. Then, with time against him, he hurried to get ready for training.

"The field" was a patch of grassy land a hundred or so yards long, located behind the Big Sky Drive-In. In addition to the thick lines of trees that flanked the old theater, the clearing was made even more private by the gently rolling hills on its other sides. Alex stood with the rest of the Beta Team in the middle of the field as rain poured from the sky. He projected a flat surface of energy above their heads, sending rain cascading in a perfect square around them. Across from the Betas, the High Council was at one edge of the field, as was Misty, who enjoyed watching the weekly occasions when the Betas trained as a group. Everyone on the sideline held large black umbrellas, giving the row of Cloak members a somewhat funerary look, the sound of water pelting nylon filling the air.

Shade and Barrage stepped forward, standing before their young troops.

"If you're to be successful as a team, you'll need to work together as one, playing to one another's strengths," Shade said, addressing the group.

"To do this, you must know the possibilities of each of your teammates' powers, but also their weaknesses," Barrage said. "Today you'll get a taste of this. You will be split into two teams. Note that there is an umbrella located at each end of the field."

He motioned to the black umbrellas, rolled up like black spikes, shoved into the soggy ground at either end of the clearing.

"Each team will be responsible for both defending their

own umbrella and stealing that of their opponents. The first team to open their opponents' umbrella wins. The umbrella can only be opened physically, meaning that Alex, you won't be able to do it using your powers."

"Capture the flag," Titan said.

"Exactly," Shade said. "It is not our intent to have any casualties or serious injuries today. Don't take it easy on your opponents, but remember that your enemies in this exercise are still your brothers and sisters in Cloak."

"Misty," Barrage said, looking over his shoulder. "Front and center."

Misty, standing beneath Phantom's umbrella, was dumbfounded. She looked up at her aunt, who nodded to her. Misty smiled, and she presented herself in front of Shade and Barrage.

"Yes?" she asked, eager to be included.

"Your training has progressed well," Shade said. "The rest of you may not be aware of this, but Misty has recently demonstrated the ability to move not only large objects in her sublimated form, but people as well. In our training session earlier this week, she was able to transport one of our Unibands from one room to another. Soon she will make a valuable addition to the Beta Team."

Misty could hardly withhold her excitement.

"There are five silver balls about an inch in diameter located on the field," Shade said to Misty. "Your goal is to collect all of these before either of the teams has won. You are not to interact with the other players, but will need to defend yourself against stray attacks that may be slung your way. Do you understand?"

"Yes, ma'am!" Misty said.

"All right, then. Misty, you'll start in the center of the field. Alex and Mallory will defend the north umbrella together. Julie and Titan, you'll take the other one." She motioned to opposite sides of the clearing.

Alex smiled, and allowed his telekinetic umbrella to shrink, exposing Titan and Julie to pouring rain.

"Seriously?" Julie shouted. Titan didn't flinch.

"Go now," Shade said. "To your flags."

"Defeat them," Barrage growled in his low, grinding voice. He winked at his children.

"We'll split up," Mallory said to Alex as they hurried to their assigned side. "I'll take Titan. He's got a low tolerance for temperature changes. Julie should be easier to take care of with your mind anyway."

"You sure, Mal?" Alex asked. "Titan will probably be playing dirty."

"Of course he will, but I have a feeling he'll go easier on me. Just remember, Julie always attacks without thinking. Prey on her weaknesses and we'll be fine. If you see a hole, make a run for it. I'll try to lay down as much cover fire as I can."

"Ready?" Shade yelled when each team was in position. "Begin!"

The two teams sprinted toward each other as rain pelted their faces. Misty looked around at the Betas all racing toward her and began to disintegrate, floating up into the air and out of harm's way. Titan barreled straight toward Alex, his long legs and enhanced strength sending him hurtling down the field like a cannonball, while Julie ran at his heels, talons out and low to the ground. They were going to try to double-team him, Alex thought. Luckily, Mallory had no intention of letting that happen, and a subzero ball of energy flew through the air, leaving behind a trail of flash-frozen raindrops. It nailed Titan in the right shoulder, knocking him off his course and causing him to slip and fall with a heavy groan.

"Nice!" Alex said, but Mallory was too focused on a follow-up attack to respond.

Julie jumped over her brother without skipping a beat, eyes still focused on Alex. She began weaving, running in a scattered series of directions. She crouched and dug her long claws into the soggy ground every few steps, slinging clumps of mud and gravel at Alex.

"Good!" Barrage yelled. "Take advantage of your environment."

Alex tried to focus on her directly, but between the rain and her erratic movements and the earth flying at him, he had a hard time getting ahold of the energy around her. As she closed in, she leaped at Alex, and he managed to push enough force her way so that her clear, razor-sharp fingers missed his chest.

She landed in a crouch in front of him as he grabbed at his shirt, searching for cuts. He backed away with wide footsteps, putting some distance between them.

"Nonlethal attacks, Julie," Shade yelled angrily from the sidelines.

"Are you crazy?" Alex asked. "This is training. You almost gutted me!"

"Stop whining," she said. "We're here to win."

Alex narrowed his eyes and summoned a jet of mud from a nearby puddle that hit Julie in the face, causing her to flail about blindly, shrieking in disgust.

Somewhere behind him he could hear Misty laughing.

Julie slipped around on the swampy ground, her hands returning to flesh as she wiped the mud from her eyes, but Alex knew she'd be pouncing as soon as she had a chance. Before she could regain her footing, he concentrated on making a force field like the one he had made in training the day before, only this time it was around Julie, trapping her inside instead of keeping bullets out. His adrenaline was pumping, and he poured that energy into a shimmering dome around her. She ran toward him, but quickly hit the inside of the invisible bubble, knocking herself back.

Julie, realizing that rain was hitting some unseen barrier around her, began dragging her talons across the energy field, shouting something about fairness that Alex couldn't quite make out.

Keeping Julie trapped took all his concentration, though, and Alex had momentarily forgotten about his sparring teammates. By the time he realized that Mallory was flying straight toward the containment bubble, it was too late for him to stop her, and she smashed through, landing on top of Julie. Alex turned to find Titan running toward him.

"I'll take over with him," Alex yelled to Mallory. She nodded, radiating so much heat that rain was turning to steam before it ever hit her shoulders.

Alex turned his attention toward Titan. Mallory had clearly gotten some good shots in. Frost had collected on one of his shoulders. His right thigh and most of his left side were burned, exposing the layer of metal underneath his outer coating of skin. He looked like some sort of android charging at Alex.

"Stop him," Alex muttered to himself, regretting the switch of opponents. "You can do it."

He tried creating a series of force fields in front of Titan, expecting them to stop him in his tracks, but the speeding juggernaut smashed through them as if they were made of paper. Frantic, Alex poured all his telekinetic energy into a single miniature bubble and sent it soaring toward Titan's chest. At the same time, Titan leaped into the air, flying almost horizontally at Alex: a six-foot blond bullet.

Alex's aim was true, though; the bubble caught Titan's shoulder, slowing him down. The metal boy landed on one knee a yard in front of Alex, and was on his feet in a split second, smirking.

"We know you're off the team," Titan snarled. "You're pathetic. You always have been. And when this is all over with, you'll be nothing more than the servant to my High Council."

Before Alex could reply, Titan rushed forward and head-butted him, sending him straight to the ground, his head fuzzy and ringing. And with that Titan was off, sprinting toward Alex and Mallory's umbrella. Alex rolled over onto his stomach, watching Titan run. He glanced around the field: Mal and Julie sparred, Misty disappeared and reappeared every few seconds, and on the sidelines, his father's expression was stern. But it was his mother's face that got to him. She looked sad. Disappointed. And he knew exactly what he needed to do in order to make her proud.

He returned his gaze to Titan, who was closing in on his prize. Alex clenched his teeth, glaring at his opponent, and allowed his emotions to take control. Rage was fueling him now. In a single motion, he pulled Titan back, hoping to just slow him down. Instead Titan was flung backward at an impossible speed, sailing through the air. His heavy body flew over Alex and landed in the middle of the field, skidding several yards in the mud, creating a long divot in the earth.

Alex was determined not to let Titan get back on his feet again. He rushed to the metal boy's side, lording over his opponent. Still focusing on Titan's body, he pushed down on it with his mind. Titan shook his head, trying to figure out what was happening as Alex pressed him down farther into the earth.

Everything else in the world seemed to have stopped moving. Alex took all the feelings of anger and shame and poured them into his powers. He could see Titan's eyes bulging, his breath labored. And it felt so good to see Titan squirming under his power.

Alex allowed his gaze to drift to the sidelines, where an odd thing was happening. Barrage was trying to make his way onto the field—but Shade had her hand on his shoulder, pulling him back. Her eyes flashed, and the man stopped trying to struggle. On her face was a smile so pure that Alex could hardly believe it. His lips curled back, and he grinned to himself as he stared at Titan, who had by now sunk several more inches into the ground.

"Your eyes . . . ," Mallory said. She and Julie had come up to his side and were staring at him in bewilderment.

Alex looked back down at Titan and saw his own reflection in the metal showing through Titan's stomach. His eyes were blazing, energy crackling and shooting from them, like they were balls of lightning. The stronger his powers were getting, the wilder they became—and the more others were noticing them.

"Alex?" A soft, frightened voice came from his right.

It was Misty. Her face was scrunched in fear as she stared at him. She took a step back as he met her eyes, and then disappeared, turning into a colorful haze of dust and floating with exceptional speed away from the field. Five silver balls were left behind, falling to the earth with thick plunks.

Alex realized what he must have looked like. A mighty being, yes. But malicious. Without mercy. He was doing exactly what his mother had talked about earlier. He was proving that he was the most powerful weapon of Cloak. A force to be feared.

He released Titan, who immediately sat up, gasping for air. Julie rushed to his side. Titan tried to stand but fell back into the imprint of his body in the earth. He stared up at Alex, equal parts rage and terror in his eyes.

"Perhaps that's enough for today," Shade said, stepping her way onto the field. She held four cylinders under her arm and was passing them out before anyone could react to Alex's display of power.

"These are blueprints of Justice Tower based on the best information we were able to gather," she continued. "Study them. Memorize them. Know everything about them."

After leaning down to hand a cylinder to Titan, Shade stood before Alex and held the final one out to him.

Welcome back to the team, she whispered into his head before turning and walking away. The High Council followed her off the field, leaving Alex alone with his teammates in the pouring rain.

Titan stood up, wobbling at first. He shook off Julie's attempt to help as he trudged back toward their home. His sister followed him.

"I guess that means we won," Mallory said tentatively.

"Yeah," Alex replied, his voice shaky. "I guess we did."

Shade had been right that morning: He was getting stronger. But at the same time, Alex had the distinct feeling that he was beginning to lose control.

12

FALLEN
RANGERS

Alex threw himself into studying the blueprints for Justice Tower alongside his teammates, memorizing the layout. The structure was located on the edge of Sterling City's museum and cultural district, a few miles north of Victory Park. It was only fifteen stories high—a far cry from the skyscrapers dotting the southern end of Victory Park—but it rose above the other buildings in the area. It was cylindrical, all light-colored limestone and mirrored glass that reflected the Texas sun. The twelfth story was a single room with a 360-degree view of Sterling City, the walls made up entirely of tempered glass and support beams, where the Rangers could look out over the city. But the iconic part of the structure was the opaque glass dome that capped off the building. At night, it burned brilliantly, as Alex had seen that weekend: a beacon illuminating the skyline, reminding the citizens of Sterling City that they were not alone.

The plans helped Alex make peace with Misty. It had taken an intricately folded bouquet of paper roses to persuade her to even open the door for him after his display of power, but eventually she let him inside her room, where they spread the plans out on the floor and looked them over together. She was quiet at first, but eventually eased back into her usual self, and soon she was jabbering at length about the new capes and sashes for Cloak uniforms that she'd designed. It wasn't until he was leaving that she brought up anything about his fight with Titan.

"Alex," she said softly. "Promise me that you won't ever change. That you'll always be you."

He smiled.

"I promise," he said, though he wasn't sure what she meant. Who else would he be?

Since Sunday's training, Titan's only direct communication with Alex had been in steely glares from across the room. Titan had spent the days after his defeat walking around the compound sulking, until Barrage finally took his son out into the country to smash through one of the abandoned shacks that dotted the Texas countryside. The two of them blew off steam in this way, and Titan seemed to be in somewhat better spirits once they returned, the knuckles on his hands shining silver from the exercise in destruction.

At the beginning of the week, Alex had decided that there was no reason for him to sneak out and travel to Victory Park again. After all, he was back on the strike team, and that had been his motivation in the first place. But as the days progressed, his conversation with Kirbie kept running through his mind, no matter how often he tried to push it out of his thoughts. She had spoken as if he had a choice in whether or not his future belonged to the Cloak Society, but she was a Ranger—she didn't know what she was talking about. Soon he'd be facing her in battle, though Alex's stomach knotted when he replaced the image of Titan sinking into the earth with that of Kirbie.

As the week wore on, he wanted more and more to talk to Kirbie one last time. He found himself wondering where she was in Justice Tower as he became familiar with its design. He'd liked how light and clearheaded talking with her had made him feel—how nice it was to speak to another superpowered person his age who had experienced the world in ways he hadn't. And he wanted to know if he would be able to see her in full color once again. Besides, though he wouldn't admit it to himself, there was something thrilling about sneaking out and gaining knowledge that someone like Titan wouldn't have.

So after dinner on Saturday night, while the other Betas

gathered in the common room to watch a movie, Alex excused himself, claiming to be tired. He went back into his room and began to prepare for another trip through the Gloom. He remembered how hard it had been to navigate Victory Park in the dark the week before and searched around for his map of Sterling City so he could review the layout and paths. Unable to find it, he sighed.

Luckily, Alex knew the Tutor was sure to have something he could use. He could stop in and borrow a map under the guise of research.

Alex walked lightly down the hallway and knocked on the metal door of the library. Immediately after knocking, he could hear the Tutor rummaging about inside, speaking loudly.

"I'll warn you now that I won't be foolish enough to accept your Queen's Gambit again tonight," he said as the door slid open. Upon seeing Alex, he stopped short. "Oh, Alexander. Good evening. I'm afraid I thought you were Gage. I'm expecting him for chess. Have you come by for a game, by chance?"

"I'm sorry to disturb you, sir. I was wondering if I might be able to borrow some materials from you."

"Of course, of course," the Tutor said, standing aside and motioning for his student to enter. "How delightful. I was just preparing tea. May I offer you some Earl Grey?"

"No. Thank you, though."

It was odd to hear the Tutor speak to him in such a casual way. He was always so dull and severe in tutoring sessions. It had never occurred to Alex that there might be something more to the man behind the stodgy beard and thick rectangular glasses.

"Straight to business, then," the Tutor said. "What are you looking into? You seemed to be quite taken by the lessons of Aristotle we covered this week. I've just finished reading a brilliant analysis of his theories on causality that you might be interested in seeing. . . ."

Before Alex could respond, the man was already scooting papers around his desk, looking for the book.

"Actually, I'm looking for something more . . . geographical. I was wondering if you had any maps of Victory Park laying around that I might look at. With everything going on . . ."

The Tutor looked up at Alex with such a stern expression that the boy forgot completely where he had intended his sentence to go. A moment of silence passed between them.

"Lying," the man finally said.

Alex was sure that he had gone white.

"What? No, I'm—"

"The maps would be *lying* around, young Knight. It's an intransitive verb."

"Oh," Alex exhaled with a sigh. "Yes, of course."

"I wondered how long it would be before one of you came wanting to know more about Victory Park," the Tutor said, speaking solemnly. "Your generation is far less concerned with its own history than your parents'. Why, your mother read every scrap of paper, every hastily jotted note about the Society's history that she could get her hands on. It is no surprise to me that her son is the one who has taken an interest in that battle, what with your family being so central to it."

"Yes, my mother has told me many times that it was my grandfather who led the charge against the Rangers."

"He was a brilliant man. It was a tragedy that we lost him that day, especially since he had been so against the battle in the beginning."

"He was?" Alex asked.

"Oh, yes. He and some of the other elders of the High Council at the time did not completely agree with the direction that the younger members were taking the Society. They felt there was no need to make such a public gesture or seek to dominate the Rangers of Justice. They were quite happy with the way things were. When they discovered that your mother and the others had commissioned the Umbra Gun, the council was furious. I suppose that old men and women like me are somewhat resistant to change, though."

"What was it that changed their minds?" Alex asked.

"I can't say for sure. In the end, your mother always did

have a way of getting people on her side," the Tutor said. He shook his head. "Now, I have a file on the Victory Park incident here somewhere. If you'll excuse me for a moment."

"Uh, thank you," Alex said. He had only wanted a map—a current map, not one a decade old—but perhaps an entire file on the park would be useful. And he had to admit that his interest was piqued.

Alex walked around the room, letting his fingers graze the spines of the books stacked everywhere. He moved around the side of the man's desk, which was completely covered in notes and reading materials (though unlike Gage's workshop, everything here was set up in an organized fashion), and picked up a tall bronze eagle that the Tutor was using as a paperweight.

"That's a finial," the Tutor said, returning. "French. Two hundred years old. It once topped a Napoleonic flag. It was a gift from your mother. I believe she picked it up the same time she procured the Rembrandt in Gage's workshop."

Alex turned. The Tutor was holding a black leather box with the words STERLING CITY PARK INCIDENT written on a card stuck to one side. The man carefully set the box down on his desk in front of Alex.

"Ah, sir," Alex said, "that says 'Sterling City Park' on it."

"Well, of course," the man said. "The park was renamed after the battle. It was almost 'Memorial Park,' but the city went with something more positive in the end. Take it.

You'll find maps in there, along with newspaper clippings and a few of my own notes, recorded for posterity. I beg you, please use the utmost care when handling these materials."

"Thank you, sir," Alex said, turning to leave.

"No, thank you, young Knight," the old man said. "It does my heart good to see you take initiative."

Alex excused himself from the library, thanking the Tutor once again for his help, and hurried to his room. He rustled through the box, found a map, and studied it for a while, refamiliarizing himself with the paths. Just after ten o'clock, he changed into his formal training gear—ready to blend into the night—and pocketed the Blackout Bomb he had left over from his previous trip to the park. He put his ear to the door and, hearing no footsteps, set out.

Alex was able to get to Centennial Fountain with little trouble, jogging at a slow pace, fighting his instinct to sprint the entire way there. Finally he was at the clearing, where he half expected Kirbie to be standing. A few birds lounged about on the fountain's edges, but they were all pigeons—no oversized golden falcons in sight.

Alex sat in front of the fountain, waiting, but quickly grew anxious. The longer he waited for Kirbie, the more time he was away from the base. He began to panic, wondering if he'd left too early in the evening, or if one of the Betas had noticed that he wasn't in his room. After fifteen minutes he took the Blackout Bomb from his pocket and held it out, studying it. He had to do something to get Kirbie's attention. If she hadn't figured out he was in the park already, surely she'd notice if the light of Centennial Fountain went out. A click, and the glowing light of the Gordian knot was gone, along with the sound of water cascading out of the bronze sculpture. He stood still, eyes to the sky, listening for the beating of wings or the crunch of footsteps on gravel.

He was so focused on watching for Kirbie that he didn't see the creeping movement of tendrils slithering toward his legs from the shadows behind him. It wasn't until they were coiled around his ankles that he noticed them at all, and before he could react, the dark cords were winding up his legs.

"No!" he breathed before they pulled his feet out from under him, dragging him into the bushes.

The memory of Lone Star held on the ground by Phantom's shadow energy flashed in his mind, and he expected to be sucked into the Gloom and back to the underground base to face the punishment of the High Council. But instead he found himself hanging upside down several feet off the ground. His palm felt normal, meaning that it wasn't Phantom's power that had dragged him away from the clearing. Bending up, he grabbed at whatever was keeping him suspended in the air. Alex could just barely make out the silhouette of wide, flat leaves. He had been attacked by sentient vines.

There was a rustling in the bushes to his left, and out of the darkness walked a figure with blond hair and soft features, wearing a Junior Rangers uniform. Kyle. Thorn. Kirbie's brother.

"Oh, it's you," Alex said gratefully, as if Kyle were an old friend.

"What are you doing here?" the boy asked, his tone accusatory.

"Nothing," Alex assured him. "It's fine. This is just a misunderstanding."

"I recognize you," Kyle said, his voice hard, but threatening to tremble. "You're one of the Cloak Society."

"I don't want to hurt you," Alex said, trying not to sound at all threatening. "I'm not here for anything bad."

"My name is Thorn, junior member of the Rangers of Justice. It is my sworn duty to protect the citizens of Sterling City. Now, what are you doing here?"

"Look, it's not what you think," Alex said. "Your sister—"

"Kirbie?" Kyle asked, his voice suddenly frantic. The vines tightened around Alex's ankles, causing him to wince in pain. "What have you done to her?"

"I haven't done anythi—"

"Where is she? If you've hurt her . . ."

"No! She's . . . ," Alex started, but he wasn't sure where to go from there. He didn't want to get Kirbie in trouble.

There were footsteps, heavy and fast, somewhere behind Alex. He twisted around, swinging, but could see only blackness in the trees. Someone was headed straight for him, and Alex tried his best to focus, preparing for the worst.

Kirbie stepped forward. She stopped short upon noticing that Alex was upside down, dangling from a tree branch.

"Alex!" she said, alarmed.

"Kirbie?" Kyle asked, his confusion warranted.

"Kyle?" She noticed her brother for the first time.

"Alex?" Kyle asked, the word beginning as a question but leaning dangerously toward an accusation by the time his mouth closed on the *X*.

"Kirbie," Alex said, relieved. "I mean, hi. Would you please tell your brother that I'm not doing anything wrong?"

"Wait . . . Kirbie, you know this guy?" Kyle asked.

"Kyle, just . . . just let him down so we can talk," Kirbie said.

"He did something to the fountain," Kyle stammered. "I haven't had a chance to check out the rest of this area, but it wouldn't surprise me if there were more of them—"

"No, it's okay," Kirbie interrupted. "I was just in wolf form, and the two of you were the only scents I picked up. Besides, I know why he's here."

"What?" the boy asked. "What are you talking about? You're not . . . *consorting* with him or anything. . . ."

"If you'll put him down, I'll—"

"We *just* fought him," Kyle said, thrusting an angry finger toward the suspended Cloak member.

"Uh," Alex butted in. "I'm feeling really dizzy."

"Kyle," Kirbie said, sternly now. "Put him down."

Kyle looked back and forth between Alex and his sister. He grimaced, and the coils around Alex's ankles went slack, dropping him to the ground with a thud. The Beta was up on his feet far too quickly for someone who had been upended for several minutes. He suddenly felt lightheaded and began to sway. He took a few steps forward, reaching out for a tree to lean on, but instead fell straight back down toward the ground. He would have landed there, too, if it had not been for Kirbie swooping in and catching him.

"Are you okay?" Kirbie asked, her arms wrapped around his chest, helping him to his feet.

"Yeah," Alex said. "Sorry. I just need a minute to recover." The concern in her voice was so genuine that it caused him to smile. Realizing that he was still half cradled in Kirbie's arms, he jumped back and leaned against a nearby tree.

"Explain," Kyle said, a finger again pointed at Alex, eyes boring into Kirbie.

"Alex is—"

"Our enemy," Kyle said, cutting her off.

"He's thinking about defecting from the Cloak Society," Kirbie continued. "And we're Rangers. It's our duty to help those in need."

She cast a sympathetic glance toward Alex.

"He's a lot like us," she said. "He just needs someone to talk to."

"It's a trap," Kyle said.

"No," Kirbie countered quickly. "I believe him."

"What are you thinking, Kirbs?" her brother asked after a pause.

"Just trust me, Kyle. Okay? Please."

Kyle looked at Alex with marked disdain, and then back at his sister, staring intently at her. Her face was insistent, but gentle.

"Okay," Kyle finally relented. "Fine. But I will be *right here*. Ready to do anything." He turned to Alex. "You got that?"

"Yes." Alex nodded. "Loud and clear."

"Thanks, Kyle," Kirbie said.

Kyle nodded and, after giving Alex one more hard look, stepped deeper into the wooded area of the park. The trees and bushes leaned away from him as he walked, closing up again as he passed through, until he was no longer visible among the plants.

"Hi," Alex said, picking leaves from his hair.

"Hey," Kirbie replied. "Are you feeling better now?"

"Yeah. I just needed a second."

"Good," she said, turning back toward the fountain. "I'm glad you came. Want to go for a walk?"

Alex followed, trailing behind her as she walked through the clearing and onto one of the trails.

"What did you do to the fountain?" she asked. "I saw the light go out."

"Nothing permanent," Alex said. "It was just a little trick with the electricity."

"Well, it's probably not a good idea to do that. It attracts unwanted attention."

"I'm sorry," Alex said. "I didn't realize anyone else would be out watching the park."

"Kyle wanted to help out tonight, and I couldn't convince him to stay behind," Kirbie said. "Don't mind him. He's just overprotective of me. He's probably the nicest person I've ever met."

"I guess I'll take your word for it," Alex said. "He's good with vines, at least."

"He's a pretty good fighter in the park where he's in his element," Kirbie said. "In the city, he's much less of a threat. I'm just thankful the grounds of Justice Tower are practically a garden. I think it makes him feel more comfortable. At home."

They continued on the path, walking side by side. Alex

didn't know where they were going, but he didn't much care. The night was cool and still.

"So," she said. "Do you own anything that's not black, or is that just how supervillains always dress?"

"Oh," he said, looking down at his dark clothes. "I'm sure I have something colorful somewhere in my closet. . . ."

"Relax, I was just kidding."

"You're one to talk," Alex said. "Is that . . . spandex?"

"No," she said, pretending to be offended. "Well, sort of. It's an extra-strong material that stretches and contracts when I transform. Trust me, it's a lifesaver."

"So can you change into any animal?"

"No," she said. "Not yet. The wolf just comes naturally. I've been doing that for years. The bird is newer. It just . . . happened. Lone Star thinks that one day I might be able to morph into anything, but that's really just a guess."

"That's incredible," Alex said. "If I were you, I'd probably never walk around looking like a normal person."

He imagined how intimidating the Beta Team would be with a hulking she-wolf standing beside them. Kirbie had gotten into the wrong line of work.

"A werewolf running around in Victory Park sounds like something out of a horror movie. Besides, I don't like to turn into that unless I have to. I don't like scaring people."

They neared a large clearing Alex had never been in before. Squinting, he could make out people silhouetted in the distance. He feared that they were walking into a trap and his muscles tightened, but once they were closer, Alex saw that the figures were lifeless, cast in a shiny silver metal that seemed to glow, despite the dull moonlight. Kirbie had led him to some sort of sculpture garden.

As they entered the clearing, Alex stared up at the men and women standing on granite pedestals, towering over him. They were locked in triumphant poses, arms raised to the sky or hands resting on their hips. They wore capes and tall boots with emblems on their chests. He counted nine of them, spaced throughout the open garden.

"Oh, wow," Alex said, humbled. "This place is amazing."

"Yeah, I know. It's packed with tourists during the day. But at night, it's the most peaceful place I know."

Suddenly it dawned on Alex where they were and who the statues around him represented. An engraved slab of black granite resting in a grassy crater confirmed his suspicions: IN MEMORY OF THOSE HEROES WHO FELL SO THAT WE MIGHT STAND. This was the site of the battle between the Cloak Society and the Rangers of Justice. He was surrounded by the people his parents had banished to the Gloom.

"No wonder the council never brought us to the park," he muttered to himself.

"What happened here changed everything," Kirbie said. "Not just for the Rangers. Not even for Sterling City. It changed the world. People across the globe had looked up to the Rangers. They idolized them. Nobody expected that in a matter of moments most of them would be gone. It certainly changed Lone Star, killing all those Cloak members at once. People remember it now as a victory on our part, a triumph for Sterling City. But back then . . . Killing goes against everything the Rangers stand for. Lone Star carries that guilt with him every day."

Kirbie pointed to two statues on the opposite side of the clearing sharing the same base. A man held a triumphant sword into the sky, while a female held a single palm outstretched in front of her.

"Those are Amp's parents. His father, the Guardian, led the Rangers. It's been tough for him. He's still angry about what happened. You can't really hold that against him, though."

"No, I guess not," Alex said quietly. He was beginning to feel the actions of the older generations of Cloak weighing down heavily on his own shoulders, and he was no longer reveling in the idea of his family rushing into battle.

"Can I ask you something?" he said. Kirbie nodded. "Were your parents there too? Is that why you're with the Rangers?"

Kirbie sat down on a park bench, cross-legged. When she spoke, she didn't look at him.

"No. I was never meant to be a Ranger. When my

powers kicked in, I was an eight-year-old in a small town in west Texas. I was a normal girl one moment, and the next I was some kind of monster. No one knew what to do. My parents couldn't take me anywhere. Who would they even take me to? Kyle's powers came around the same time, but they were different. They were invisible. They could be ignored. My parents just got rid of all the houseplants and killed our lawn. But they were scared of me. They were fighting all the time over what to do with us, trying to figure out what had caused this and whose fault it was. They never figured out why it was happening. Eventually the way they looked at us—at me—changed.

"And then one day they told us that we were going on vacation. They were taking us to Sterling City. Kyle and I were *so* excited when we packed our bags. We checked into a hotel in the big city and had a fancy room-service dinner. And I didn't turn at all that whole time, because I was trying so hard not to ruin the vacation. Then the next morning we came here. To the park. They asked us if we wanted ice cream, and of course we did. So Kyle and I played while they went to go find some.

"That was the last time we saw them. Kyle and I stayed in the park for days. We didn't know what else to do. Then one night, right here in this garden, Lone Star flew in from the sky and found us sleeping on a bench. He said that everything would be okay. That we were special and he would take care of us.

"That's why we're Rangers," she said, meeting his eyes. "It's why we're trying to make this city a better place. Because we choose to."

Alex could see her clearly now, her colors brighter than they had been before. It seemed unreal; he only dreamed in such vivid hues. He stared at her for several moments.

"Why are you looking at me like that?" she finally asked.

"I'm sorry," he said. He didn't know what else to say. "I can see you."

"Um . . . yeah. I'm sitting right in front of you."

"No, I mean . . ." He paused for a moment, trying to figure out how best to describe the way he saw things. "After I got my powers, everything I saw—everything I see—is blue. The sun, the ground, people. Everything. All tinted the same color."

"That's so sad," Kirbie said. Her face dropped. The color was fading from Alex's vision now, back to cobalt.

"Until I saw you."

"Huh?" Kirbie asked.

"I can see you in color," he said. "Not all the time, but sometimes. It happened last weekend, and again just now."

Kirbie didn't know what to say. Her cheeks flushed.

"Why do you fight? Why are you still a part of Cloak?" Kirbie asked. "I think you'd be a great Ranger."

"I'm a fourth-generation Cloak member," Alex started. "I never questioned my loyalty to them. I mean, until now," he stammered, remembering his cover. "My mother can read minds, so I learned when I was pretty little not to think about anything that might make her mad."

"The Cloak Society is a group of supervillains."

"Only because we have to be," Alex said, beginning the type of speech he'd heard from the High Council so many times. "The world turned its back on my ancestors. It forced us underground when we should have been made kings and queens. And then Lone Star killed our people. My family. What would you do?"

"Revenge is a pretty human motivation for a group that thinks of themselves as superior," Kirbie said. "Look around you. These people sacrificed themselves defending the city against Cloak. If only you could look at it from the outside, you would see things differently."

"That's easy for you to say."

"We all have the ability to decide what we think is right," Kirbie said. Her voice was full of hope. "Come back with me now. Let me take you to Justice Tower. Lone Star and the others will gladly take you in. We could use someone like you."

"You could use my power, you mean," Alex said flatly.

"No," Kirbie said. "Someone like *you*. Someone good."

Alex was silent, staring at the ground.

"I don't think I can," he said. "Cloak is my family. It's all I know."

"No," she said. "You know me. And you know how to take a stand."

She held a hand out to him, willing him to take it, to follow her back home. Alex stared at it for several moments before standing. Somehow, the lie he had told her in the shopping center had become his reality, and her words were making sense. He only had to do what he wanted. He had a choice, and he made his decision.

"I should get going," he said. "If anyone notices I'm gone, I'm dead."

Kirbie's shoulders slumped.

"I'm sorry if I upset you," she said. "You saved me. I'm just trying to return the favor."

"Thank you," Alex said. "I mean it."

"Will I see you again?" she asked. "If you stay with Cloak, it doesn't make sense for us to meet like this. But . . . I'd like to see you again. One more time? Just as Alex and Kirbie, not as heroes or villains?"

"Yes. I'd like that."

"This is my last day on park duty," she said. "Tomorrow night I can sneak out. Say . . . seven o'clock?"

"I'll be there. Where?" He didn't even stop to think about whether he'd be able to get away.

"There's an ice-cream shop on Victory Circle and Adler

Lane, on the east side of the park," she said. "Meet me there."

"Okay," Alex said. "Perfect. I'll be there at seven."

They smiled at each other, then Kirbie turned and walked toward the northern end of the sculpture garden, past the watchful eyes of Amp's parents and other fallen Rangers whose names Alex didn't know. She stopped when she reached the path and turned back to him, giving a slight wave. Alex stood in the middle of the sculpture garden, watching her golden hair bounce with each step until she disappeared into the darkness.

He knew he was getting in over his head. Luckily, the first day of winter was still months away.

Later, in his room, Alex flipped through the rest of the contents of the box the Tutor had given to him. On top was a photograph of a dozen or so members of the Cloak Society, most of whom Alex knew only from stories. In the center were Alex's mother and father, dressed in dated versions of the black-and-silver uniforms of Cloak. She had her arm around an older man to her left, Alex's grandfather. He flipped the picture over in his hand to find a list of everyone in the photo, handwritten in the Tutor's elegant script. Most every name was followed by a dash and the word "deceased." Only four names stood alone: Shade, Volt, Phantom, Barrage.

The newspaper articles were all the same. Hysteria,

shock, and, later, lengthy obituaries. TRAGEDY IN STERLING CITY PARK, one headline read. HEROES FEARED DEAD, read another. Alex tried to read each of the articles but found that doing so made him short of breath. One article listed not only the fallen Rangers, but the civilians who had died in the cross fire. Innocent bystanders that no one in Cloak had ever bothered to mention before. Alex let his finger trace their names, wondering who these people were, and who they might have left behind.

The accompanying photos were black-and-white rectangles of people crying, mourning, clumped together outside Justice Tower in unified anguish. There were pictures from tributes and memorials across the globe, and dignitaries and leaders pronouncing the event a loss for the entire world.

There were no tears shed for the Cloak Society.

13

ESCALATION

"We've called this meeting because there's been a slight change in plans," Phantom said from her seat at the head of the long, dark table. "Our attack on the Rangers has been moved. We will be taking Justice Tower in one week."

Alex felt like all the air had been sucked out of the War Room.

"All RIGHT," Titan exclaimed, slamming a palm down on the table. Beside him, Julie's eyes were wide as she began to laugh. Mallory's lips curled up, but she took the news with more caution.

"What's the plan?" she asked.

It was early in the evening on Sunday. The High Council sat on one end of the table opposite the Beta Team. Gage stood off to the side between the two generations of Cloak in his long white lab coat, a small electronic pad in his hand.

"Next Sunday, the Rangers will be guests of honor at the Mayor's Ball on the far east side of town," Phantom said. "That's when Justice Tower will be at its most vulnerable. We cannot ignore this opportunity to retrieve the Umbra Gun. As such, we're taking this time to brief you so that everyone is up to speed on the new timetable. Gage, if you would."

Gage nodded. He tapped on the electronic device in his hand. The screen on the wall across from the table flickered on and displayed a digital blueprint of Justice Tower. Alex couldn't help but notice how run-down Gage was looking. The bags under his bloodshot eyes were a deep, ominous color, and his curly black hair was sprouting unkempt in every direction.

"Based on an analysis taken during your mission at the bank," Gage said, "I have deduced that the force field surrounding Justice Tower is derived from Lone Star's light-based powers. It uses the same energy that illuminates the dome at the top of the tower and, I hypothesize, is charged by Lone Star via a specialized battery in much the same way we utilize Volt's electrical conduction to run our base. I've developed a device that negates this particular energy signature, so we can counteract its power."

"To put it plainly," Barrage said, ever annoyed by

technical jargon, "Gage has come up with a way for us to punch a hole in the Rangers' security system."

"Exactly," Gage continued. "In addition, while normal methods of scanning the building have been fruitless, based on the energy distortion the force field causes, I have been able to detect a faint trace of Phantom's energy profile here, on the tenth floor of the complex. This must be the area where the Umbra Gun is being stored." He typed a short command into the computer system and the screen zoomed in, highlighting the tenth floor in a bright shade of blue.

Alex was beginning to feel ill, though he concentrated hard on keeping his face stoic and his feelings of trepidation guarded in telekinetic energy. Everything was happening so suddenly that he hardly had time to process the information. All he knew for sure was that the new schedule left him with little time to figure out what he would do about Kirbie. He'd been playing through their conversation in his mind all day. She was now the face of the Justice Tower attack.

"We must assume that after we're in the tower, secondary security measures will be put into action," Phantom said. "We must be prepared for anything. Once inside, I should be able to transport us immediately to the tenth floor. The energy stored within the Umbra Gun will make it easy for me to detect its precise location. When found, Gage will inspect it. Right, Gage?"

"Yes, ma'am," he said. "Once I have the weapon in

hand, returning it to full functionality and making any other adjustments will be relatively simple."

"Wait," Alex said, suddenly very worried about his friend. "Gage isn't marked. If something happens and he gets shot with the Umbra Gun, he'll get lost in the Gloom. Can Phantom find him if that happens?"

"Your concern is admirable, Alex," Phantom said. "But rest assured we'll mark Gage before this mission."

Gage smiled for the first time since the meeting began.

"Gage has no battle training, so our number one priority will be protecting him until we have the Umbra Gun secured," Shade continued. "At that point, we'll head to the twelfth floor, the building's observation deck. This is the single most open area in the tower and is where we will take our vengeance on the Rangers."

"This is going to be the best day of our lives," Julie said, her fingers twitching with excitement.

"Despite what you might think," Barrage said, jumping in, "the Rangers are very intelligent. We assume our intrusion will set off alarms no matter what precautions we take, and based on the location of the Mayor's Ball across town, and the fact that all the Rangers are fliers, we estimate that they will return to the tower within two minutes of our entry. We'll be waiting for them on the observation deck. If necessary, Volt, Phantom, and I will hold them off while Gage completes repairs on the Umbra Gun. If for some reason the weapon cannot be used at that point, we will retreat, though this will be avoided if at all possible. If we leave with the weapon, they'll be expecting it the next time we meet."

"So what are we supposed to be doing while all this is going on?" Titan asked.

Barrage smiled at his son.

"The Mayor's Ball is a black-tie affair," he said. "The Junior Rangers will most likely be left behind in the tower, and, if their zeal during the bank mission was any indication, they will try to stop us once they realize we're inside their base. It will be up to the Beta Team to take them out should they try to interfere in any way."

"The Junior Rangers are young, but they're well trained," Volt said. "I think you all learned that the hard way when you faced them last time. Keep them at bay and off our backs."

"But don't kill them," Shade broke in. "I want them alive. I want to see Lone Star's face when they're sucked into the Gloom."

"Kirbie," Alex whispered. An immense amount of power welled up inside him, and it took all his concentration to keep it at bay.

His utterance had been louder than expected, though. His mother and Gage both whipped their heads over to stare at him.

"What was that, Alexander?" Shade asked, her eyes drilling into him.

"Uh . . . ," Alex said, floundering. "Kirbie. That was the name of the girl who beat up Titan at the bank."

"What?" Titan shouted, pounding his fist on the table. He looked ready to leap across and strangle Alex. "I would have had that she-wolf if you hadn't—"

"This is not the time to bicker," Shade said. "Alex is right. There's the animal girl, the Guardian's son, and—"

"The plant guy," Julie said flatly, obviously still seething over the fern that had bested her at the bank. "He's mine."

"Do not let your desire for revenge get in the way of strategy," Shade said. "We are a team, Julie. Remember that. Though it's true your talons are likely the best suited for taking on the boy's creations. Titan, your target is Amp. He's the oldest among them, and with your bulk you should be least susceptible to his sonic blasts. Mallory, you'll provide cover for the both of them. And Alex, you showed last weekend that you are quite adept at taking on close-range fighters. We'll need that against Kirbie. The girl is no threat if she can't get near us. Use your telekinesis to keep the little animal at bay."

"Of course," Alex said.

"I realize that this is a lot to take in," Phantom said. "But we will be discussing this further as the attack draws near. I've been impressed with your progress these last weeks. I assume that I don't have to tell you how important this is for each of you, and for the future of Cloak."

"What happens after?" Alex asked.

The room was silent. Everyone turned their heads to stare at the boy.

"What do you mean?" Phantom asked.

"Well . . ." He was choosing his words as carefully as he could. "We've been focused on defeating the Rangers for as long as I can remember. After they're gone, what happens then?"

"Alexander," Shade said, her lips spreading into a slight smile. "If we destroy the Rangers, then the city—the entire country—knows how strong we are. They'll realize quickly that defying us would be cataclysmic. We'll establish ourselves as the new law in charge of Sterling City. Our nonpowered brothers and sisters have been accumulating all sorts of political and economical clout in the past decade to smooth this transition. You'd be surprised how quickly the human mind will pledge its allegiance when promised wealth and power. From there, we'll amass allies and plan our next course of action."

"The time following this mission will be the greatest era that Cloak has ever known," Phantom said. "Leave the planning to us. We will guide you. Gage, we need you to stay for a few moments. The rest of you are dismissed. The High Council is in for a long night as we finalize the details of this assault. Find yourselves a good dinner and get some rest. Until further notice, all your academic lessons are canceled. Starting tomorrow, you will live and breathe this mission. For the glory."

"Hail Cloak," the Beta Team said in unison.

They parted, hurrying off on their separate ways once they reached the second floor. Titan and Julie made a bee-line for the kitchen, but the thought of eating gave Alex a feeling of nausea. He needed to be alone with his thoughts and figure out what, if anything, he was going to do about Kirbie, who he was supposed to meet in an hour.

Mallory followed Alex as he walked down the hall of the Beta wing.

"Can I talk to you for a second?" she asked, stopping him before he could enter his room.

"Mal. Sure. What's up?"

"Alone?" she asked, even though the two of them were the only ones in the hallway.

Alex was confused but opened the door to his room and gestured for her to follow him inside. He took a seat at his desk, swinging his chair around to face Mallory.

"What do you think about this?" she asked.

"It seems like a good plan, I guess," Alex said. This was true; the plan was smart from a strategic standpoint.

"Do you get the feeling there's something they aren't telling us?" Mallory asked, her voice almost a whisper.

"What do you mean?"

"I don't know," she said, grimacing. "I understand that this is about revenge. Everyone is mad about what happened at Victory Park. I get that, and I want that too. But will defeating the Rangers really cause so much damage to the city?"

"I don't get what you mean," Alex said.

"I shouldn't be talking like this . . . ," Mallory said, shifting her weight. She was obviously uncomfortable with the conversation, which made Alex all the more interested. He nodded, urging her on. "Well, you asked it yourself . . . *then what?* Are we making an announcement on the news that the Cloak Society is now in charge? They keep telling us that this will usher in a new age of Cloak as rulers, but they've never mentioned exactly how we get to that point."

Alex thought back to his mother's glory speech about how the golden age of Cloak was upon them. It had roused images of archaic hedonism in his mind, like something out of a Greek myth. Now it occurred to him for the first time that maybe there was something else in the works.

"It's just like the bank mission," Alex said, thinking out loud. "We thought it was a reward for us—my mother told me it was a birthday present—but the diamond was for one of Gage's projects."

"They needed to see how we'd do in actual battle and to distract the Rangers while Barrage and Gage analyzed their building," Mallory added. "None of which we knew until after the fact."

"Right."

"Which makes me wonder what we haven't been told about *this* mission," she said.

"You have a point," Alex said, shaking his head. "I don't know what they're going to do."

"Me neither," she said. "But I'm guessing it's probably something big. This attack is only the beginning. Everything's happening so fast. I'm still trying to wrap my head around it."

"I'll talk to Gage," Alex said.

"Yeah, that's a good idea. Let me know if you find anything out," she said, moving toward the door. "I'm going to grab dinner. Want to come?"

"Huh?" he said. She hadn't yet left and already he was sinking into his own thoughts. "Oh. No. I'm not hungry. Thanks."

"Okay. I'll see you later," Mallory said.

With a rush of air from the sliding door, she was gone, her footsteps barely audible from the hallway.

Alex had so much to think about that he wasn't sure where to begin. His meeting with Kirbie was fast approaching. He wanted to warn her of the terrible fate that waited for her in one week, but that meant the betrayal of his friends and family. He had to choose between the two: between his birthright and the unfamiliar feelings conjured up by a girl he hardly knew. Not only feelings toward her, exactly, but toward the world at large. She thought he was good. She thought the Rangers could use him as a *person*, not just as a tool. That he was more than just a weapon.

Kirbie had been right all along. He *did* have a choice. But now he wished he didn't have that responsibility.

He tried to weigh his options rationally. He could perform his role in the attack on Justice Tower, facing Kirbie in combat and fighting for Cloak as he was born to do. But the thought of going up against her made Alex feel short of breath. Besides, Mallory had been right. He suspected there was more to the capture of Justice Tower than the council was telling them, and if his mother's talk of the world cowering before Alex was any indication, he didn't even want to consider what Cloak's next move would be.

Of course, he could always tell Kirbie what was going to happen. But then what would he do? Go back to the base, carry out the mission, and act surprised when the Rangers were waiting for them in a week, the Umbra Gun destroyed? What if Mallory or his parents got hurt? And if Cloak was able to escape, would he stay with them, gearing up for another assault, and give up contact with Kirbie?

Alex's head was beginning to ache. He rubbed his eyes and shook his head, unwittingly releasing a mild wave of telekinetic energy that rocked the lighter objects in his room. The box that the Tutor had given him earlier slid across the floor, smacking into his closet door. Alex stared at the container, remembering the pictures inside. The obituaries. The city in lamentation. The twisted faces of mourners. It was no longer a box of his proud history, but proof that the world would fight them. That taking over wasn't as simple as the council made it out to be. That maybe Cloak was wrong. He thought of the sculpture garden, of Amp's parents. Of the figure lost in the Gloom. And he imagined the look that Kirbie would give him as the energy released from the Umbra Gun covered her body. Could he live with himself if she too became a skeletal wretch in the Gloom? A sculpture in Victory Park?

For now, Alex had to get out of the base or he'd miss Kirbie completely. He walked over to his mirror and, patting down his hair, realized that he was again wearing all-black clothes. He dug through his dresser until he found a T-shirt that looked lighter than the others, one Misty had given him a few months before. He threw it on and walked out the door, trying his best to be quiet. With any luck, the council was still meeting down in the War Room. He breathed a sigh of relief when he found the elevator empty, and pushed the button for the first level.

He stopped just a few feet from the open doors to Gage's workshop. Gage was inside, hunched over something mechanical, a soldering iron in one hand. He had goggles pulled down over his eyes and looked intently focused on whatever creation was on the table in front of him. Alex tiptoed past the wide entryway.

"I'm happy that you are here," Gage said just as Alex was halfway across the open space. "I have something for you."

Alex froze midstep. Gage turned around and stared at Alex through the thick goggles. Maybe it was just the soldering iron in his hand, brandished like a dagger, but Gage looked uncommonly intense.

"Oh, I . . . ," Alex said, fumbling over his words. "I was just dropping in to see what you were up to. And to talk about the meeting today. It's really exciting, right? Especially since you'll be going with us."

Gage set down his tool and motioned for Alex to come inside.

"I am looking forward to finally having a chance to inspect my father's invention up close," Gage said, pushing his goggles to the top of his head. "I can't say that being so near combat is appealing, but I'm happy to be of service."

Alex nodded, nearing his friend.

"I built you something," Gage said, handing Alex a rectangular steel box with black rubberized corners. A series of buttons were located on the top, and one side appeared to be an electronic screen. "It's an alarm clock just like your old one, only this one should be virtually indestructible."

"Wow," Alex said, feeling suddenly very guilty for even

entertaining the idea of betraying his best friend. "Thanks."

"Don't mention it. Think of it as a belated birthday gift."

The two of them stared at each other. Gage inspected his friend's expression, and Alex tried his best not to appear anxious.

"Well, I should be going," Alex finally said. "You look really busy, and I've got a lot of work to do before tomorrow."

"Yes," Gage said as Alex turned away. "I've been trying to figure out how exactly my father managed to tame Phantom's power. Inspecting the transporter configurations has proven most useful, though I am in no way ready to build anything so complex myself. Still, it's an impressive system, wouldn't you say?"

Alex exhaled. Gage knew that he'd been sneaking out. There was no use trying to lie to him.

"How long have you known?" Alex asked.

"Like I said, I've been studying the readouts. The link between the base and the safe house is one that is rarely used, especially late at night. But traffic has been up lately. It wasn't until the Tutor told me that you had visited his library asking for maps that I realized it was you."

"Have you told anyone?"

"Of course not," Gage said.

"It's just so stifling down here . . . ," Alex offered.

"This has to do with the Ranger girl, doesn't it? This is about Kirbie."

Alex looked away, but was silent.

"Do you have any idea what the council—what your mother—will do to you when they find that you have been sneaking out to consort with the enemy? We are preparing to *attack* them." Gage's voice was threatening to become far too loud for such conversation.

"Be quiet, Gage," Alex said, his eyes shifty with paranoia.

"You are walking an incredibly thin line, Alex. Why would you risk everything for something like this?"

"Because she's a friend," Alex said. "And because I'm not sure I agree with what we're doing. What we're *planning* to do. Do you ever ask yourself why you're here? Why you're working for Cloak?"

"For the memory of my father," Gage said.

"The Rangers didn't kill your father, Gage. *Cloak* killed your father. He worked himself to death after what happened in Victory Park. And now you're doing the same thing. Have you even slept this week? You're going nonstop to help a bunch of people who treat you like you're a second-class human."

"It's because I don't have powers."

"Gage, look around you. There are weapons in this base that are decades ahead of anything people in the outside world have dreamed of. Same with our security system. And with our computers. And you are *twelve years old*. If that's not a superpower, I don't know what it is."

"My father would have wanted me here," Gage said. "He devoted his entire life to Cloak, and it is my duty to pick up where he left off."

Alex couldn't hold back any longer. Every doubt, every question raised in his mind over the last week came spilling out.

"What if he was wrong? We should be worried about math tests and gym class, not whether we are going to survive a battle, or if we have what it takes to destroy the life of someone we don't know, just because our parents say that's what we're supposed to do. How do we know they're right? Tell me you haven't wanted to be a normal kid."

"But we are not normal," Gage said.

"Okay, fine. But tell me you haven't wondered what it's like to be looked up to instead of treated like a tool. Like a servant."

Gage cringed at the word. Alex softened his tone.

"Someone called me a good person recently. And it felt nice. I think you are a good person too, Gage. And rational. Maybe we're just here because we're afraid of leaving. Or because we pretend that we don't care, or don't know what's going to happen. I've seen what happens to people in the Gloom, and I don't think I could live with myself if I sent Kirbie there. Maybe it's time we stopped doing things for our parents and started doing what *we* think is right."

"Not just Kirbie," Gage murmured.

"What?"

Gage's eyes fell to the floor.

"The prototype I've been working on," he said, speaking quietly. "It's an accessory to the Umbra Gun. When attached, it changes the flow of energy. Instead of shooting a single round, it releases all the stored energy at once. It becomes a sort of bomb capable of spreading Phantom's energy out over a large area, transporting anything it touches into the Gloom."

"How large of an area, Gage?" Alex asked, his voice shaky.

"It's untested but . . . I estimate a three-mile radius."

"That's impossible," Alex said, refusing to believe it. "You don't know how the gun works."

"The gun was never the issue," Gage said. "It was the harnessing of Phantom's power I couldn't replicate. I assure you, the bomb works."

All at once, everything made sense to Alex. If Cloak destroyed an area that large in a single attack, the entire world would tremble before them. No one would be able to stop their rise to power, because everyone would fear that at any moment they might do it again.

No. Alex wouldn't let it happen. He couldn't let Cloak banish so many people—so many unknowing people—to the Gloom. He had to tell Kirbie. He had to warn the

Rangers. Betrayal was the only option. Slowly he backed away from Gage.

"You are going to meet Kirbie now, aren't you?" Gage asked quietly. "You're going to warn her about the attack."

Alex said nothing.

"I wish you had not told me," Gage said grimly. "I'm sorry that I called you in here tonight. Your mother is a telepath. You may have found some way to keep her out of your mind, but I haven't. One stray thought, one misstep, and she will—"

Clang. Near the entrance, something metallic fell to the floor. They both turned, startled to see Titan at the end of a long workshop table. He stood there, a soda in one hand, staring at the two boys, looking intrigued. In front of him, one of Gage's inventions was scattered in pieces on the floor.

"Dude, Gage, this place is a mess," Titan eventually said, taking a sip from his soda can.

"Titan, hey," Alex started. How long had he been standing there? "We were just—"

"Yeah. Whatever. I don't care. Gage, my dad is waiting to see you in the War Room."

"At once," Gage said, hurrying over to his desk and gathering notes.

As Gage shuffled through his cluttered workstation, Alex and Titan looked at each other. Alex shifted his weight and pretended to be interested in the alarm clock Gage had built for him. Titan stood still, a slight smirk on his face, his eyes never leaving Alex, even as he brought his drink to his mouth. Alex could feel his gaze, and it took all his restraint, every time the boy lifted the aluminum can, not to crush it.

Gage paused beside his friend. He stared at Alex, long and hard, then nodded slowly.

"Good-bye, Alex."

"Good-bye, Gage."

There was something about the way Gage said good-bye—as if he knew it was the last time they would see each other.

Alex suddenly felt cold. Alone.

Gage walked toward the exit. Before leaving, Titan turned back to Alex and smiled.

"What's the matter, Knight?" he asked. "You look pale."

"I was just thinking about how you must have felt when I was crushing you last weekend," Alex retorted.

"Ha. Right."

And with that, Titan was gone, and Alex was left standing alone in Gage's workshop. The young genius had been right, of course. It was only a matter of time before Alex's mother caught him off guard and she was alerted of his betrayal. Alex realized then that if—when—he told Kirbie, he could never go back to Cloak. He would have to leave, getting as far away as possible from his mother and Phantom's ability to hone in on the skull branded on his right palm. He would have to say good-bye to his life, to his teammates, to Sterling City forever.

Alex hurried back to his room, where he tore a few of the clippings and photos off his wall—his grandfather's picture, the family portrait, a Polaroid of the Beta Team taken a few months before their first mission—and shoved them in his pockets. In the bottom drawer of his desk was a small box full of cash he'd saved up over years of Thursday outings. What he needed was more pocket space. He threw open his closet door and took out the dark gray trench coat he'd been so excited to receive not two weeks earlier. His eyes lingered on the two silver bands on either shoulder. He slipped his fingers beneath them and ripped them off, one after the other. He stuffed his money in the coat pockets and carried it under his arm.

He was about to leave, when he caught sight of his origami animals, all pushed up against the wall from the wave of energy he had let loose earlier. He thought for a moment that he could see them in color, but he couldn't be sure of that with the frenetic state of his mind.

He wondered if he should get Mallory and try to convince her to leave with him, but he couldn't risk it. He thought of Misty, too. Maybe he could save her, could keep her from growing up to be someone like her aunt Phantom. But if he had to go on the run, he wasn't sure he could take care of her. He didn't know if he could bear to see her as an outcast. He couldn't be responsible for her life.

Alex gathered up all the paper animals from his desk and, cradling them in his hands, walked outside. As he tip-toed down the hall, he let them fall, guiding them through the air behind him, so familiar with the design of the hall-way, the place he had lived his entire life, that he could direct the animals to their new home without even looking over his shoulder. They came to a stop in front of Misty's door, resting there on the cement. A paper menagerie. He hoped that she would understand that he cared. And he hoped that she would forgive him for leaving.

14

BETRAYAL

With every step he took toward Sterling City, Alex reminded himself that he was making the right decision. He *had* to tell Kirbie what was going on. He even kept his eyes open in the Gloom as a reminder of what he was saving her from, though he saw no spectral figures this time, only the cold, dark expanses of a world he hoped he'd never again have to visit. He cut through Victory Park. The light of the setting sun cast a peaceful aura around the place. The air was cool, even in his Cloak trench. Alex wondered if the Umbra bomb would reach the statue garden, or Centennial Fountain, or even the gravel path he was rushing down.

It was seven fifteen by the time Alex made it to the other side of the park. He could see Kirbie sitting at a table outside a corner shop, surrounded by chatting customers, pushing a napkin-wrapped paper cup back and forth on the table in front of her. She stirred a spoon around in it with a slight frown. For a flash she appeared in full color again, wearing jeans and a red zip-up hoodie over a white shirt. A canvas messenger bag was at her feet, held in place by green sneakers with white rubber caps on the toes. She was a vision of colors for Alex, a masterpiece of golds and pinks and reds and greens.

Jogging across the street, Alex caught Kirbie's eye. Her lips curled up in a wide grin as he approached.

"I didn't think you were going to show," she said.

"Sorry," he said as calmly as he could manage. "I just got held up."

"Is everything okay?"

"Yeah," he lied. "I've just got a ton on my mind right now."

"Do you want to talk about it?" she asked.

"Not yet," he said, taking a seat.

He realized then that he hadn't thought about how he should break the news to her. It wasn't something you just blurted out. And deep inside, he was terrified that once she knew what Cloak was planning, she would hate him for it.

He stared down at the table. Maybe he could start by telling her that he was discovering that he had no ambition toward conquering and fearmongering. Or that he felt more comfortable and better about himself when talking to her than he ever did at the underground base. Maybe it would be better to start with that before he explained that soon Cloak would be at Kirbie's doorstep, ransacking her home with the intent of destroying her and everyone she loved, and then part of the city.

The table began to shake.

"Um, Alex?" Kirbie asked, trying not to sound worried, "Is that you?"

"Oh," he said, not even realizing that his powers were in use. "Sorry."

Kirbie stared at him, her eyebrows furrowed together. He hated to see her looking at him like that. "Hey, you want to see something?" he asked, seeing a chance to raise her spirits a little. "Give me your napkin."

She nodded and handed it to him. He cupped his hands around both sides of the napkin, partly shielding it from passersby. It was a rectangle, a blank white paper canvas. He stared at it, focusing his power on it until the edges began to move rapidly, folding in on one another. He heard Kirbie take in a short breath of air. The napkin moved so quickly that it was almost a blur, Alex pouring all his concentration into it. Before Kirbie knew what was happening, an intricate paper flower was sitting on the table, small and delicate.

"Here," Alex said, sliding it across to her.

"Thank you," Kirbie said, her voice soft. "This is incredible, Alex. Wow."

"Listen . . . ," he said. "I need to talk to you about something."

"Okay, what?"

He stared into her eyes, and a shadow passed over her face. He wanted just a few more minutes before they talked about the future.

"Not here," he said. "Do you want to walk through the park? We can head toward Justice Tower."

"Okay," she said wearily. "But you're kind of freaking me out."

They walked in silence through the park, watching their silhouettes grow long on the ground. At first they passed people regularly, but the farther they walked, the fewer people they met on the paths. The park was dangerous once night fell, after all. Terrible things happened there, people had heard. Minutes ticked by, until they were once again in front of Centennial Fountain, the heart of the park, by now deserted by tourists. It was at that point that Kirbie could not take the suspense anymore.

"Whatever you have to say, you can tell me," she said.

"You're not going to like it," Alex said, stopping and turning to her. "Just promise me that you'll try to understand. Or at least that you won't be too mad. This is me trying to do the right thing, okay?"

"Alex?" She was looking worried, preparing herself for the worst. "What's wrong?"

Alex stared at her face, the stunning mixture of concern and care, an expression he had rarely seen in his lifetime. Telling her about Cloak's plans would set into motion a series of events that could easily tear them apart for good. He wanted to stop time in some way, to live in that moment as normal kids, with no worries in the world.

"A lot has happened in the last few weeks," Alex said, his face grave. "And it feels like I'm seeing things clearly for the first time in . . . well, maybe ever."

He paused, meeting her eyes.

"I think of you as a friend," he said.

"Oh. Is that what it's taken you all night to say?" Kirbie smiled, sighing with relief. "That's great. I've really liked getting to know you too. I'd like it if—"

"No, that's not it. I mean, it is, but there's something else. Something about Cloak."

"What is it?" she asked, her posture stiffening.

Alex opened his mouth to speak, when he felt his arm start to tingle like a sleeping limb coming back to life. The sensation quickly concentrated itself in his right palm, which began to freeze. He stared down at it. An inky skull was forming there, spewing dark energy.

"No," he muttered.

"Alex?" Kirbie was starting to get frightened now, and she

reached a hand out to him. "Are you okay? What's wrong?"

"Run," he said, his body shaking.

"What?"

"Get out of here. NOW!"

Kirbie glanced at his palm, realized that something terrible was happening, and leaped into the air, taking her bird form. But she was clumsy, her wings getting caught up in her normal clothing, giving her a troubled start. Her shoes fell to the ground, socks ripping apart.

She flew only a few yards before a purple crackle of electricity shot from somewhere in the bushes and caught her, just as she was beginning to rise above the treetops. An anguished call shrieked from her open beak as she began to fall. With each second passing, her body became less birdlike, until she landed in her human form on the ground beside Centennial Fountain with a sickening thump.

"No!" Alex shouted, running toward Kirbie. A pained groan escaped her lips.

Alex recognized the electric energy, of course. It was the unmistakable power of his father, who now stood in the trees off to the left of the path, beside Barrage. Had Alex remembered his training, he would have sought cover and identified his enemies, but he didn't even bother to glance in their direction. All he cared about was Kirbie, lying motionless on the ground.

Before he could reach her, two more figures rose out of

the shadows, cutting him off. The darkness fell away from them like smoke drifting into the air. Phantom and Titan.

"Sorry to interrupt your evening," Phantom said, her voice a sickening mix of anger and self-satisfaction.

The Cloak Society—his teammates and family. They were dressed casually, in T-shirts and button-downs and jeans—the same things they had been wearing at the meeting that night. They must have left at a moment's notice. Alex knew there was no way he could take on the High Council. Besides, with Phantom so close by, she would have him sucked into the Gloom before he could even get Kirbie off the ground.

"So it's true," his father said, staring him down.

"I can explain," Alex said, his mind racing, trying to figure out the best course of action.

"There will be no need for that," a voice from behind him said coldly.

Alex felt hands on the sides of his head. His mother's lips were at his ear. It was all over now.

"Sleep," she whispered.

The last thing he saw before blacking out was Titan, picking up Kirbie and slinging her over his shoulder. As Alex's eyes closed, the metal boy looked back at him and smiled.

15

WEAPON OF
CLOAK

When he opened his eyes, Alex could see Kirbie across from him, in a white room on the other side of a huge window. She was seated in a blocky steel chair riveted into the cement floor. Thick metal bands covered her wrists, ankles, and chest. On a table at the back of the room, her messenger bag and its former contents—pens, books, what looked to be a Rangers uniform—were stacked neatly, as if recently cataloged. He instinctively started to move forward, only to find that wide metal cuffs bound him, too. Alex was restrained in the same sort of chair. Nothing made sense to him. He was disoriented, woozy. His watch was partially covered by one of the restraints, but he could see that only a few hours had passed since he'd been in the park with Kirbie.

"Don't bother struggling," his mother's voice came from behind him. She walked around his chair slowly, the tapping of her boots echoing through the room. She had changed into her mission attire; the three silver bands of the High Council gleaming on the shoulders of her trench coat. "You may not recognize these rooms—we've been using them for storage since you were a child—but I assure you that they were designed to imprison people far more powerful than you."

"Mother? It's . . . hard to . . ." Alex felt like he was stuck somewhere between sleep and consciousness.

"To concentrate, I imagine. I'm running a low-level psychic disturbance through your head right now. Nothing damaging. Just think of it as a little static."

"Kirbie . . ." He looked back at her through the window. Her eyes scoured the steel-and-concrete room. She fidgeted, trying to find a weak point in her restraints.

"She can't see you," his mother explained. "Or hear you, for that matter. For all she knows, you planned this. You led her on with your moonlight walks and origami flowers just so we could get a chance at her. That was your original intention, was it not? Well done."

"No—I—"

"Oh, my Alexander," she said, walking up to his side, placing her hand on his cheek. "How far you have fallen.

I assume I don't have to tell you how disappointed I am. What shame you've brought your family. To think that you would betray your own flesh and blood after all that we've done for you."

"Are—are you going to kill me?"

His mother chuckled as if he had suggested the most preposterous thing she could imagine. She was in a much more amiable mood than he had seen her in for a long time, which added to his confusion—and worried him immensely.

"Of course not. You are still my child, Alex. You can be rehabilitated. You would be surprised how easy it is for someone like me to shape the mind of another person. To erase things. Feelings. Memories. To make you forget this conversation, for instance." She turned to Kirbie. "Or that a person ever existed. Cling to her memory while you can, son. Because I assure you, it is temporary."

"You're lying," he said. Inside his head, he was trying to raise his mental barriers, attempting to concentrate enough to at least think straight.

"Ah, there it is. That blue safe where you keep your private thoughts. I wondered what you had hidden from your mother in there." She sighed. "I had so hoped that you would mature into the man you were meant to be. I wanted you to become Cloak's next leader by your own accord. But I see now that I have been too lenient on you."

"What are you going to do to Kirbie?"

"I'm going to do what's best for Cloak," she said matter-of-factly. "The Mayor's Ball is an opportunity that would have given Cloak the upper hand, but that's nothing compared to what is sitting in there. That girl possesses knowledge about the Rangers and Justice Tower that we would never be able to find out on our own. I'm going to learn everything she knows, and when I'm done, I'll strip her mind, cut away her memories, and turn her into something we can use. She'll be a pile of clay, ready for me to mold. She is powerful, I'll give her that much. And she has fight in her. So don't worry. You two will be serving Cloak alongside each other soon enough."

"No!" Alex shouted as loudly as he could. "You can't do that. She's too smart for that. She's better than that. You . . . you can't."

"Oh, poor Alex," Shade said, patting the top of his head. "You talk as if I've never done this before."

Even in his drowsy state, pieces began to fall into place. The gaps in his memory. The way she talked of stripping someone's mind. The unquestioning loyalty of the fleet of Unibands living on the first floor. He thought back to all the times he had seen her touch someone's arm in seeming affection, each time her eyes flashed for a moment. He thought of the nanny he couldn't remember, and Mallory's absent childhood. He was horrified to think of what his mother might have done to them.

"Now you're just trying to flatter me," Shade smirked. "As powerful as I am, I doubt I could manipulate minds as strong as Barrage's or Phantom's for very long. Still, I may have urged them in directions to my pleasing now and again. I have never enjoyed manipulating anyone within Cloak— or at least none of our brothers and sisters of the Umbra. I'm surprised that you didn't realize before that Mallory's history with Cloak was suspect. She was a child of defectors, of a nonpowered member not much younger than me who ran off with a commoner from the city. They tried to hide from us, tried to keep the baby a secret. But in the end, the Cloak Society always wins. It is true that they died in a fire. But that had nothing to do with Mallory's powers.

"As for the nanny you don't remember," she said, picking at a fingernail, "I suppose I was a bit jealous of how much you had taken to her."

Alex shook his head, trying to push his mother from his mind, not wanting to listen. He had to get free somehow. He couldn't let this happen to Kirbie. He had to save her.

"There is no way you're getting out of here, Alex. You are helpless. Your mental blocks are fragile. You still need training. But don't worry: Mother is here to help."

Heavy parts were moving within the door to Alex's left. After a series of clanks, the thick metal slid open, and Alex's father entered, also dressed in his mission gear, black and silver and imposing. He dragged Gage in with him, bound in shackles that encased his hands entirely in metal. Beneath his right eye was a swollen welt.

"Oh no . . . ," Alex murmured.

"We're ready," Volt said to Shade. He looked to his son but said nothing.

"Then let's not waste any time," she said, walking toward the door. "This is for your own good, Alex. I hope the two of you enjoy the show. For the glory."

"HAIL CLOAK," Alex screamed, but not of his own accord. His voice was under his mother's control, shouting so loudly that his throat burned. The door slid shut. His parents were gone.

"Are you injured?" Gage asked.

"What happened?" Alex asked weakly, shaking his head.

"Titan must have been standing behind us long enough to hear that you were going to meet Kirbie," Gage said. "As soon as I entered the War Room, Titan whispered to his father, who sent him away. While I briefed Barrage on the progress of my work, Titan returned with your mother, who was searching my thoughts before I realized what was happening. I assume after that it was just a matter of showing up in the park and scouring the area. I fear my service to the High Council has come to an end."

"But they need you," Alex said. "You're the only one

who can make sure the gun works correctly."

"She's been in my head," Gage said grimly. "Shade knows everything I do about that gun now, and I've hardly thought of anything else for weeks. They were only ever taking me as a contingency measure."

Alex's stomach cramped, and for a moment, he was afraid he might be sick. He pulled himself together as best he could and spoke.

"Gage," he said. "I never should have dragged you into this."

"No," Gage said. "You have helped to open my eyes."

"Can you get us out of here? We have to figure out how to escape before they hurt Kirbie."

"The poetry, of course, is that these restraints are of my own design," Gage said, nodding toward his hands. "They're terribly flawless. The room itself is my father's work, locked electronically from the outside. I could possibly get you out of the chair if my hands were free, but the door is six inches of steel and titanium. The glass is bulletproof. I am afraid we're stuck."

"If I can just get my head together," Alex said, "maybe I can undo the lock with my powers."

"Forget it. Even if you could sense the inside of the mechanism, the lock itself is rigged. One wrong move and this room fills with an incapacitating agent and we are unconscious for the better part of a day." Gage motioned with his bound hands to the small vents lining the top of the walls.

"So we're helpless," Alex said, looking back up at Kirbie. "My mother was right."

The door inside Kirbie's cell slid open. Shade and Phantom stepped in slowly, flanking the girl, who was straining against her bonds. Alex could hear the sounds in the other room piped in from speakers somewhere in the walls. He wanted to cry out of frustration. This was entirely his fault, and all he could do was sit and watch.

"Good evening, Kirbie," Shade said, circling the girl's chair, taking her time with each calculated step. "I've just been through a crash course in my son's extracurricular activities, most of which have to do with you. You're very clever, leading him on like that, trying to turn him over to your side. Does it pain you to know that when we're through with him, he'll be completely devoted to us?"

"Leave Alex alone," Kirbie growled through clenched teeth. "He doesn't deserve this."

"Alexander was born to serve our cause," Shade said. "His gift is extraordinary. My son will grow to be the most powerful weapon we have. He will help us show this world that *we* are its destined leaders—to be feared and obeyed. Nothing you do or say will get in the way of that."

"You're no different from every other second-rate loser the Rangers have put in prison," Kirbie said, struggling against the chair's bonds. Her hands began to morph, becoming more clawlike. Phantom, standing off to the side, saw this and smiled maliciously.

"I wouldn't do that if I were you," she said. "Transforming causes mass to redistribute itself throughout your body, does it not? Against these metal bands, you'd snap half your ribs if you tried to turn right now."

Kirbie became still and stopped morphing, but her expression remained indignant and full of rage.

"You're wondering if we're going to kill you," Shade continued, walking closer to the girl, "but I assure you that you and your wonderful powers are of far more use to us if you are alive."

Shade leaned in close to the girl's ear.

"You see, unlike your parents, I recognize potential when I see it."

Kirbie's eyes bore deep into Shade's, her lips trembling with anger.

"Now," Shade said, smiling, "let's see if you can't be of some use to us tonight."

"I won't tell you anything," Kirbie growled.

"Oh, that's sweet, dear," Shade said. She stroked the girl's hair. Her eyes were staring through the one-way mirror, as if she could see her son in the other room. "But you won't have to say a thing."

Alex watched in horror as his mother's eyes turned a gleaming, metallic silver and Kirbie's head fell back. He cried out, but no one in the other room could hear him. Energy sprayed weakly from his body, but in his current confused head, it was nothing more than a breath washing over his cell. Gage looked away, closing his eyes.

Shade's face was raised toward the ceiling, painted with a look of pure ecstasy as she plumbed the depths of Kirbie's mind. The psychic interrogation lasted for less than a minute, at which point her eyes went back to normal. Kirbie remained unconcscious. Alex's mother braced herself on the back of the chair, raising a hand to her temples and rubbing them as if her head ached. She needed a moment to process the information she'd just stolen from Kirbie's brain. She needed to figure out how to proceed.

Phantom knocked on the door, which slid open again, allowing Barrage and Volt to step in. Volt was immediately at his wife's side. She smiled at him and threw her arms around his neck, elated. Such happiness did not bode well for the future of the Rangers of Justice.

"What's going on?" Barrage asked, becoming impatient. "What have you learned?"

"In all likelihood, the girl won't be missed for several hours. Morning, maybe," Shade said. "But her brother knows of her meetings with Alex. Once they realize she's gone, they'll be looking for us and will expect that we're planning to come after them."

"The Rangers know we have a telepath," Phantom

said. "When they realize we have one of their own, they'll restructure their security measures. All our work will have been for nothing."

"Yes, but thanks to our young captive, I know how to disable their current secondary security system," Shade said. "Barrage, what's the status on Gage's prototype for the weapon?"

"Complete," the man said. His face was beginning to light up with pure delight. "It's ready for a test run."

"Go get it, and the device tuned to negate Lone Star's energy," Shade said. She turned to Volt. "Assemble the Beta Team. We're taking Justice Tower tonight."

"What about Alex?" Volt asked.

"Leave him," Shade said, pushing him toward the door with her fingertips and staring through the one-way glass. "Let him think about what he's done. I'll deal with them when we return."

And with that, they were gone, the door sealed shut once more.

Alex was speechless. All he could do was stare at Kirbie through the glass. At least she was alive, he thought. And even though he was horrified by the plans his mother had for them, for a moment he wondered if everything would work out in the end. Maybe it wouldn't be so bad, the two of them allying together under Cloak. If neither of them had any memory of their history together, maybe it could be a sort of fresh start, all the anxiety of the past washed away. They could protect each other, learn to fight for the same goals—could *rule* alongside each other.

No. It wasn't right, any of this. He had to find a way out. He had to save her.

"What are you thinking?" Gage asked from behind his friend's chair, where he was inspecting the restraints.

"If I can get that door open, you can get us out of here, right?" Alex asked. "While everyone is gone?"

"Well, yes, but perhaps you were not listening earlier—"

"I have to do something. Even if we end up gassed and unconscious or whatever. I can't just sit here."

"Okay," the young genius said after a moment. "But I want you to know now, in case something happens and we don't remember any of this later, that I'm sorry for how this has turned out. You were right to question Cloak. We cannot stand in the shadows of our parents."

"This isn't your fault," Alex said. "Now, cross your fingers. I'm going to see if I can feel out this lock."

"Alex, you know me well enough to know that I am not a superstitious individual," Gage said. He managed a small smile. "But I'm crossing my fingers as best I can within these metallic confines."

Alex nodded to his friend and turned his head to the door. He was feeling more put together since his mother left, at least, but Gage had been right: The door was solid and sturdy. Alex could sense its density. There was no way he could pull it open using his powers. He closed his eyes and tried to feel out the inner workings of the lock, slipping his telekinetic energy around the mechanics. The pins and levers and rods were seemingly endless, and his thoughts were still somewhat blurry from his mother's interference earlier. He was finding it difficult to concentrate. His controlled energy was becoming more and more erratic, bouncing around inside the mechanism recklessly. He tried to keep it together, to move the blue around with finesse, but he feared it was too late for that.

"Oh my," Gage said. "It would appear that you have triggered the gaseous element."

Alex opened his eyes and looked up, letting the energy within the door dissipate. A heavy black and red and purple cloud was drifting through one of the vents, hovering above them.

But the cloud didn't disperse throughout the room, nor did it enter their lungs. Rather, it drifted slowly to the floor, where against all reason it began to form solid matter. First fuzzy purple slippers and black leggings, then a familiar plaid skirt. The black fabric and silver bars of a Beta Team mission top came next. And finally, green eyes, red hair, and the freckled face of a ten-year-old girl.

"Misty!" Alex said. "Oh thank you, thank you, thank you."

Misty stared at Gage and Alex, her mouth agape. It was apparent that she had been crying and was confused about why her two best friends were being treated like prisoners.

"I didn't know what to do," she said, near hysterics. "Volt called the Beta Team. He said they were going on a mission. And Titan said that the two of you were locked up, but I didn't believe him. And then they all just left me and I didn't know what was going on, but I figured if it was true and you were locked up, then you might be in these rooms. I remembered them from when I first got my powers and got lost and spread out in the base before I figured out how to put myself back together. I had to come make sure you guys were all right."

"Misty, it's okay," Alex said, trying to calm her down. "You did a great job finding us. Now, I need you to take Gage with you and go back to the hallway. He's going to get me out of here."

"What? I can't do that. What's going on?" she asked. She looked around, noticing Kirbie sleeping in the next room. "Wait, who's she? Why is she here?"

"We can explain that later," Alex said. "Right now I need you to take Gage and use your powers to get him to the other side of the door."

Misty stared back at him, shaking her head.

"No. I don't like taking other people with me. I've only done it in training. What if he gets hurt? I'm not good enough. I'll figure out another way to get you guys out of here."

"Misty, I've seen you do this with things twice as big as Gage," Alex said. "Just concentrate! All you have to do is—"

"No, Alex. She is correct," Gage said, interrupting. "Misty can't sublimate another person safely. It's beyond her power." He paused. "But *the Mist* can, right? The Mist can take me to the other side of that door."

Misty's eyes were wide. She looked back and forth between Alex and Gage before taking a deep breath.

"You're right," she said, putting up a strong front. "The Mist can do this. No sweat."

Gage looked at Alex.

"We will see you momentarily," he said. Then, turning to Misty, he added, "If you would, please leave these hand-cuffs behind."

Misty nodded, her face already scrunched in concentration. Reaching out and placing a hand on Gage's white sleeve, she closed her eyes. Slowly her body started to drift away, as if it were a sand sculpture caught in the breeze. Once she was nothing but multicolored dust, Gage began to disintegrate as well, starting where Misty's hand had been on his arm, traveling rapidly over the rest of his body. The boy looked at Alex one more time, nodding as his face began to fall apart. The two joined clouds hovered in the air before shooting toward one of the vents at the top of the room. After a few seconds Alex was alone, his only company a pair of handcuffs sitting empty on the floor in front of him.

On the other side of the glass, Kirbie was waking. Alex watched her eyes flutter open, and saw her confusion in coming to consciousness locked up in an unfamiliar place.

"Hold on," Alex murmured. "I'll get you out of here."

Mechanical parts moved somewhere in the seat below him; Gage had worked quickly. The metal bands of his chair all snapped open, and Alex was up in no time, standing in front of the door. It slid aside, revealing a familiar hallway. The cells were located on the bottom floor, tucked behind the War Room. Gage was standing beside the door, a wall panel opened up to reveal a mess of wires and circuits.

"Gage, get Kirbie's cell open," Alex said. "I need to think about what to do next."

With his mother gone, the haze in his head had subsided. Before he could start to sketch out a plan, a fist rammed against his back.

"You were going to leave me, weren't you?" Misty yelled. "That's what all those animals were for. You were going to leave and never come back. Weren't you?"

"Misty . . . it's complicated," he said.

Misty was starting to cry. Alex wrapped his arm around her neck and drew her in close. At first she resisted, but it didn't take long for her to give in to the hug.

"Listen," he said. "That girl in there is one of the Rangers of Justice. . . ."

Misty gasped, but said nothing.

"I know you think she's our enemy," Alex continued. "But she's my friend. Right now, Cloak is on their way to her home to hurt her friends. They're going to hurt her brother."

"Are you going to try to stop them?" she asked, her face contorting in fear.

Alex exhaled slowly, nodding.

"Yeah," he said. "I have to."

Before Misty could protest, Gage cleared his throat. The door was opening.

A monstrous roar came from inside the cell. Before any of them could react, a blond-haired beast was in the hallway, growling like a cornered animal. With the back of her clawed hand, she swatted Gage out of the way and locked eyes with Alex, who had stepped in front of Misty. The little girl screamed, and Alex could feel her dissipate behind him.

"Kirbie!" Alex screamed. "It's me. We're here to save you."

The she-wolf growled again, her eyes showing reluctance to believe Alex. After a few seconds she began to shrink down into her human form. She took a few steps forward but began to stumble, raising a hand to her head.

"It's okay," Alex said, catching her before she dropped face-first onto the concrete. "Take it slow. These are my friends. This is Gage," he said, motioning to the boy on the floor. "And this is . . . Misty, get ahold of yourself."

Misty was still a hovering mass of particles a few feet away. She pulled her body back together and sheepishly waved at the new girl.

"How were you able to escape from the chair in that room?" Gage asked curiously, picking himself up off the ground. "I hadn't released the bonds yet."

"I'm a teenage superhero," Kirbie said, still clutching her head. "Escaping from restraints and the best way to be kidnapped were two of the first things I learned as a Ranger. Now, where are we?"

"We're in Cloak's base," Alex said. "Underground. Outside the city. Kirbie—"

"What are they going to do?" she asked, cutting him off. "That woman . . . she was in my head. . . ."

"That was my mother," he said, feeling somewhat ashamed. "There's a weapon in Justice Tower that has the power to take down the Rangers. Cloak is going after it. That's what I was trying to tell you in the park when they showed up."

Kirbie's eyes met Alex's, a tempestuous mixture of fear and anger and disappointment that made him feel worse than he'd thought was possible.

"Kyle . . . ," she said. She stood and began to take a few steps forward before turning back to Alex, realizing that she had no idea where she was. "We have to get over there. We have to warn them."

"It's too dangerous," Gage said bleakly. "If we're anywhere near there when that bomb goes off—"

"Bomb?" Kirbie interrupted.

Gage looked to Alex, as if he felt it best that his friend explain the situation.

"They're going to set off a special bomb that will transport anything in the blast zone to another plane of existence," he said. "A place called the Gloom. Just imagine hell and that's it."

"How big is the blast zone?" Kirbie shuddered to ask.

"Anything within three miles of Justice Tower," Alex said softly.

"A blast like that will take out half the cultural district," Kirbie said. "Not to mention the park, the apartment buildings . . . there are schools and hospitals in its range."

She trembled with anger and fear. Her features grew more animal.

"Somebody get me to Justice Tower," she growled.

"We'll use the transporter to take us close to the park," Alex said. "It's not too far from there."

"Great. Let's go," Misty said.

Everyone turned to stare at her. She stood with her fists clenched, as if ready for action.

"It's too dangerous," Alex said.

"No," Gage said. "Misty's right. We can't leave her here with them. You heard what your mother had planned for us. Imagine what will happen to Misty once they find out she's the one who helped us escape."

"Yeah! Plus, I can help. Look what I did with Gage!" Misty said, her confidence apparently having grown tenfold in the past few minutes. Alex wanted to think about this more, but they were wasting time.

"Okay," he said. "But you're not going up in the tower. Let's get out of here."

"Give me ten seconds," Kirbie said. "I'm right behind you."

Alex nodded, and they jogged around the corner to the elevator.

"Can we do this?" he asked Gage, holding the door back and waiting for Kirbie.

"If we are lucky, and the Rangers have put up a fight, then we may have enough time to stop the bomb. There will be a short delay between the time it's set and when it goes off. Cloak will need to get out of the area themselves."

Kirbie followed the sound of their voices and ran into the elevator, now dressed in her Rangers uniform. She'd need to be able to transform quickly.

"Let's do this," she said, pulling her hair back into a ponytail.

Alex hit the button, sending them shooting up through the compound.

"The first floor will be full of Unibands—Cloak staff— but if we're lucky, the council left in a hurry and didn't alert anyone else of our . . . situation," Gage said.

"And if they're waiting for us?" Kirbie asked.

"Be prepared to transform and run," Alex said.

There was a beep, and the door slid open. The area in front of the elevator was busier than normal, with a dozen Unibands milling about. Alex picked up the words "attack" and "Justice" out of the noise before everyone fell silent and looked at the people stepping out of the elevator: Alex, the battered inventor, the Ranger of Justice, and the little girl in slippers. Everyone stood quietly for a moment, none of them sure what to do. Finally Alex stepped forward.

"Well?" he hissed, his voice full of anger. "Don't you all have jobs to be doing?"

There was a slight pause, and the Unibands scattered.

"Nicely done," Gage whispered.

They ran down the hallway with haste, stopping only for a few seconds at Gage's workshop so he could pick up a few weapons and whatever tools he might need to disarm the bomb.

"We'll go in twos," Alex said as they entered the transporter room. "Misty, take Gage. We'll be right behind you."

Misty nodded and grabbed Gage's arm. The girl took a deep breath and shoved her right palm into the inset black box. Darkness seeped up over her shoulder.

"What's happening?" Kirbie whispered as she looked on, more than a bit alarmed.

"I wish I could say it isn't as bad as it looks," Alex murmured. "Misty, make sure you keep your eyes closed the whole time, okay?"

Misty nodded as the shadows overcame her and flowed onto Gage. Within seconds, they were sucked inside the wall.

Alex reached out his left hand to Kirbie. She took it without hesitation, and they stepped forward to the black box.

"Don't be afraid," Alex said. "Try to relax and breathe. It's going to be cold, but it will be over before you know it. Just keep your eyes closed. And whatever you do, don't let go."

"Okay," she said. "I'm ready."

Alex thrust his palm into the box. The icy darkness flowed up the arm of his trench coat, sliding across his chest. Kirbie took in a shocked breath when the freezing energy met her hand. Before she could say anything, the two of them were gone.

16

THE
BATTLE
FOR JUSTICE TOWER

On the other side of the transporter, Kirbie gasped for air, doubled over and shaking. Alex fumbled against the wall, trying to find the panel that would let them out of the dark room and into the safe-house closet.

"What was that?" Kirbie asked between gasps. "What just happened?"

"That's where a chunk of the city is going if we don't stop the bomb," Alex said.

He pulled her out of the dark room and through the closet, into the sparsely decorated living room where Gage and Misty were waiting beside the open front door. They both looked shaken, but ready.

"Let's go," Alex said, heading out into the basement.

"Once we're topside," Gage said, following him, "find a vehicle. I can manually bypass the ignition interlock. It should take less than a minute."

"Huh?" Misty asked.

"He's going to hot-wire a car," Alex clarified, climbing the steep steps that led to the street exit, leading the way. He poured thoughts into the lock on the wrought-iron gate at the top of the stairs, trying to jimmy it open. A few steps away, he gave a final push, intending to unlock the barricade but instead sending the entire door, hinges and all, flying out onto the sidewalk.

"Oops," he muttered.

They poured out of the stairwell, and Kirbie ran immediately to the center of the street, orienting herself and looking for signs of chaos in the distance. Over the trees of Victory Park, she could see Justice Tower. It was still standing, but something was wrong. The twelfth floor—the observation deck—was flickering with colors and lights, as if some sort of spectacular show was being staged inside. The Rangers of Justice were locked in battle with the Cloak Society. But there was still time.

"We have to help them. Now," Kirbie said, turning to the others. She kicked off her shoes in preparation. "I can fly one of you there."

"Take Gage," Alex said. "He knows the Umbra Gun and the bomb attachment. He can stop it."

"No," Gage said. "You go. I'll be useless in combat. Besides, I am not marked. One shot from the Umbra Gun and I'm lost in the Gloom. Stall them. We're right behind you."

"Guys, there's a truck right there," Misty said, pointing over Alex's shoulder.

"Perfect," Alex said, starting to run toward the truck. "I can—"

One of the truck's windows shattered, interrupting him. He turned to see Kirbie, standing by a sidewalk planter that was now missing a brick from its side.

"Leave them to it," she said to Alex. She turned to Gage. "Hurry."

Kirbie was already transforming, the arms of her suit peeling back as her limbs morphed into giant wings.

She flew into the air, circled around, and clamped her talons onto Alex's shoulders. He gasped as they took to the sky. In any other circumstance, he would have marveled at the sweeping view of Sterling City, the trees racing by beneath his dangling feet, the building lights blurring into streaks of blue as they flew. But his mind was firmly locked on the tower ahead. Small explosions could be seen inside, accompanied by reflections of purple energy and sudden, searing bursts of pure white light that must have been coming from Lone Star.

As they drew closer, a twelfth-floor window shattered

and a figure clad in black flew into the night, a thick vine wrapped around his waist. It was Titan, who thrashed about and tried to pull himself back inside using the vine as a rope, but it began to shrink in size and snapped, sending Titan plummeting toward the earth. He shouted a garbled curse as he fell, then hit the ground with a tremendous *clang*, the cement cracking for yards around him.

Titan was down, but Alex doubted that was permanent. He was close enough now to see inside the tower, and his eyes widened as he tried to take in as much of the scene as possible before he was plopped into the thick of it. On the west side of the room, Kyle hid behind a veritable wall of overgrown, moving houseplants. Mallory was wrapped up in heavy vines that she'd frozen solid, and Julie dodged blasts of sound from Amp. He wore jeans and a plain white undershirt—clearly Cloak had caught them by surprise.

Kirbie let out a shrieking call from her beaked mouth and flew through the broken window. She dropped Alex, who landed crouched on one knee. Transforming in midair, she was her human self by the time her feet touched the ground, already running. She called over her shoulder to Alex.

"I have to help my brother. Find the gun."

The ground was covered in bits of debris, the white marble floors scorched and pockmarked. Pillars ringing the center of the space were missing hunks of stone. On the east side of the room, Lone Star was taking on Phantom, Volt, and Barrage. He flew with incredible agility, making the most of the high ceilings and dodging their attacks. Bright beams of light shot from his hands, threatening to incinerate his opponents. All four of them were looking the worse for wear, with tears and rips and smoking holes in their uniforms. Lone Star's cape had been reduced to shreds, with scorched scraps hanging from both shoulders.

The other two adult Rangers were notably absent from the fray.

Pieces of splintered wood lay scattered about the center of the room, remnants from the table where the Rangers held meetings. On the north side, opposite Alex, was an elevator bank, near a golden staircase that connected the floors above and below. And there, scowling at him beneath gleaming silver eyes, stood Alex's mother.

ALEXANDER!

The word roared in his head. Around him, all the combatants, both Cloak and Ranger, flinched as his name rang through their minds as well. Heads spun toward him. The members of the Cloak Society looked down at him with disgust, except for Mallory, whose face was a mixture of pleading and confusion. Kirbie, in her wolf form, used the moment of distraction to toss Julie across the floor and make her way to Kyle.

"I thought you had him under control," Barrage yelled at Shade. "Take care of your son!"

It was then that Alex noticed what was in his mother's hands. He recognized it from Gage's sketches. The barrel was thick and connected to a rectangular box—the storage container for the dark energies that served as its ammunition—that was dotted with electronic displays. What appeared to be a metal rib cage was snapped to the top of the box, giving it a skeletal look. On top of the attachment, something shimmered brilliantly. It was the Excelsior I, the diamond that Alex had helped Cloak steal weeks before. A perfect thermal conductor, Gage had said.

Shade fired the weapon at Alex, and a glowing orb of dark purple mass exited the barrel, accompanied by a low, deep electronic sound. It flew toward Alex, and he dove to the right, throwing himself to the ground while pushing energy toward the bullet. He managed to knock it from its trajectory just enough so that it flew past him and splattered against a window. The tempered glass went dark before appearing to liquefy and fall away into nothing. A blast of wind shot in from outside.

But hitting him was probably never Shade's intention. Alex's head now buzzed with static. He turned to see his mother, arm outstretched and pointing at him, her eyes shining. She was trying to incapacitate him, or at least throw him off enough that he was unable to use his powers to their full ability. And it was working. Alex was finding it hard to think, even to stand. Shade smiled and turned her attention—and the gun—back toward Lone Star.

Alex made it to his knees just in time to see Mallory sliding across the floor in front of him, thrown across the room by one of Kyle's vines. The boy was still behind his plant defenses but was yelling at Kirbie, who traded slashes with Julie in the middle of the room.

"Lux and Photon are gone," Kyle shouted, frantic. "They did something to them. They just melted away and disappeared."

Kirbie loosed a deafening howl into the air and leaped at Julie. Meanwhile, Mallory was beginning to pick herself up off the floor.

"What's going on?" she asked Alex. "Is it true? Did you betray us?"

"Mallory," he said. "You have to listen to me. You were right. There's more to this attack than—"

Before Alex could finish, a small, glowing red ball rolled in front of him. Alex and Mallory instinctively jumped away, just ahead of the explosion and shower of marble dust. Barrage ran toward Alex, raising a burning hand as if to strike, but a blast from Amp knocked him to the floor.

There was a great burst of Lone Star's light from across the room, followed by the sound of Phantom screaming.

"Don't make me destroy you!" Lone Star shouted at Volt and Phantom. It was odd for Alex to hear him sound so unrehearsed. Unable to save his teammates, the hero was faced with the same situation he'd been in a decade earlier. He might have to kill once again.

Lone Star roared, flinging his arms out wide. His fists blazed along with the starburst emblem on his torso, until all three shot forward in a blinding current of light, knocking Volt and Phantom backward onto the ground with terrifying might.

"Yes!" Kirbie yelled from across the room. She was human again, standing over Julie, who struggled to get up from the ground. "Lone Star, you have to get the gun. If you don't—"

A long golden pole—part of the railing from the stairway—swung from behind the wall of Kyle's plants and smacked Kirbie in the back of the head with a clang. She fell to the floor, disoriented, fighting to remain conscious. Titan stepped out from behind the leaves and branches and vines, dragging Kyle behind him. The impact from his twelve-story fall had left large patches of his metal under-skin exposed. Titan looked over at Alex and smiled, delighted to see him there. He tossed Kyle onto the floor a few yards away from Kirbie and ran toward Amp.

The pain in Alex's head grew as his mother increased the force of her assault on his mind. Her voice started to chant in his head. *For the glory of the Society, I will grow mighty and strong. For we were born to rule the weak, and right a world that's wrong. Hail Cloak.*

"Enough," Shade yelled at Lone Star. She pointed the gun in his direction. "What do you say we finish this now?"

"You will not win this day," Lone Star shouted, his body burning brightly. "I stopped you before, and I'll do it again."

"You are a formidable opponent," Shade said, squinting her eyes against his powers. She turned the barrel of the gun to point at Kirbie, still attempting to recover across the room. "But she's not, is she?"

"No," Lone Star said, his baritone voice brittle. "She's just a child."

Shade smiled.

"What do you think?" she asked. "Can you make it there in time to save her?"

Shade didn't give him a chance to respond. She pulled the trigger without ever taking her eyes off Lone Star, but her aim was true. A bass sound reverberated through the room as the gun expelled a mass of Phantom's concentrated energy. Lone Star moved with such speed that he was nothing but a glowing blur passing before Alex's eyes, a rush of wind and light that reconstituted in front of Kirbie just in time to catch the impact of the shot in the center of his back.

Lone Star fell to his knees. His body glowed bright as he attempted to fight off the energy slowly seeping over him, but it was no use. It spread, inch by inch, over his torso and down his legs, making its way up to his face, which was contorted with pain. Kirbie, horrified, reached her hand out to him.

"Stay back," Lone Star said, gasping. His eyes were desperate and his body shook.

"No. No, you have to fight it," Kirbie said, her lips quivering. "Make it stop."

"Get the others and run," Lone Star said through strenuous breaths. "Don't let them take you."

"No, please," she said, pleading with him as if he had any choice in the matter.

"Stay true, Kirbie," he whispered. "You've made me proud."

The dark, oily power washed over Lone Star's face, entering his mouth and shooting down his throat. He arched his back, parting his lips in a silent shout. His body began to melt away into nothing more than an inky pool. It slid across the marble floor, into the shadows, where it disappeared, sucked into the Gloom. Lone Star was gone.

Across the room, the Cloak Society stood quietly. Shade stared unblinking at the spot where the leader of the Rangers had just stood. Slowly her body began to tremble, and Volt rushed to her side. She was laughing. It was a hysterical, uncontrollable reaction to a lifetime's work finally paying off. She looked around at her fellow Cloak members. There was no need for words. They were beaming.

A primal scream sounded from across the room—Amp

vibrated with anger, channeling sound energy, preparing to unleash a sonic boom. A simple, quick burst of Volt's purple electricity dropped him to the floor.

"You're monsters," Kirbie said, her voice shaking. "All of you."

"Says the little wolf girl." Shade laughed, hardly able to speak through her frenzied celebration. Behind her, the rest of Cloak was regrouping in front of the elevator bank. "And I had such high hopes that you would be joining our cause. It seems for the best that we just put you down here and now."

Alex wanted to scream, but his body and brain would not cooperate. The energy built up inside him, like a kettle threatening to boil over, but despite his best efforts, he was unable to overcome his mother's interference. He crawled to his knees and slowly made his way across the floor, but Kirbie and the rest of the Junior Rangers were too far away. There was no way he could make it there in time to save them.

"Eeny, meeny," Alex's mother said, alternating her aim with each word. "Miney . . ."

A bolt of energy flew through Shade's shoulder from behind, sending her hunching forward, screaming out in pain. As she fell to the ground, Alex saw Gage at the staircase, a laser pistol in hand. Misty peeked out from behind him. In their elation, Cloak hadn't noticed the two of them sneak in.

Gage looked as shocked by his actions as the rest of the room. A high-pitched scream from Misty brought the inventor back to his senses as Julie lunged at the two of them, claws first. Misty wrapped her arms around Gage's waist and closed her eyes. They disintegrated immediately, and Julie landed on the ground, sliding into the side of the staircase.

Kirbie got to her feet and hobbled over to Kyle, who was staring at the Cloak members across from him, shaking.

"It's okay. Try to get up. We have to go," she said. But he was in shock and barely responded.

Gage and Misty reconstituted beside Alex.

"Are we all that's left?" Gage asked. "Did they get Lone Star and the others?"

Alex nodded, blinking his eyes as he stood. The static in his head had suddenly disappeared. The laser shot had broken his mother's hold on his mind, and he was feeling better with every second.

"The bomb prototype is attached," Gage continued. "But it doesn't appear to be activated yet."

"Take care of Misty," Alex said, staring down his mother, who was inspecting a smoking hole the size of a dime in her left shoulder. "I'm getting that gun."

He stood and walked toward the High Council and the Beta Team standing in front of the elevator bank. The energy he'd been gathering while his mother had been blurring his thoughts poured out of him with each step. His emotions ran rampant, and his powers were raging.

"Are you going to beg us to take you back?" Julie asked. "You can start by bowing."

"What do you expect to do now, take us all on? You and the crying Kid Rangers in the corner? It's over," Titan said from his sister's side, watching Alex walk toward the center of the room.

Alex could feel his mother's thoughts pressing against his, but he was ready for her this time. He wrapped a thick shield of telekinetic energy around his mind. Shade's silver eyes grew wide as her thoughts slammed against his mental blocks, her head flinging back at the power of her son's defenses. She smiled broadly, standing in the center of the group.

"So angry," Shade said as her eyes returned to normal. They took on a kind, warm appearance as she stared into her son's. "I've trained you well."

"Do you know what happens now?" Alex asked, looking over his mother's shoulder at his fellow Beta Team members. "They're going to use the Umbra Gun to send part of the city into the Gloom. I'm talking about thousands of people gone in an instant. Is this what we've been training for? Is that what our birthright is? We're not running drills or playing capture the flag anymore. This is murder."

"So?" Titan snorted. "They call us supervillains, you

idiot. How will they ever respect us if we don't live up to their expectations?"

"The sacrifice is for the greater good," Phantom said. "The reign of Cloak will turn Sterling City into a paradise. Petty crime, murder, theft—all ended."

"A paradise for us, but that's all," Alex said. "You don't care about the city or the people. All you care about is power. And revenge."

"Son," Volt said, his fingers twitching with electricity at his sides. "Stand down."

"Mallory," Alex said, pleading now, "you can't be okay with this. I know you. And if you had any idea how much my mother messed with your mind. . . . They killed your parents, Mal."

Mallory's face grew pale, but she didn't move.

"Will you please shoot him already?" Julie asked.

Shade stepped forward. It was the end, and everyone in the room knew it. The Junior Rangers were all but defeated, and Gage and Misty were poor excuses for soldiers. Their only real opponent was Alex, the boy who had spent most of the battle cowering on the floor, unable to move. The boy who time and again failed to meet expectations or control his powers properly. Whose conflicted allegiance and inability to take action would be his downfall.

"Poor Alexander," Shade said, raising the gun's barrel to once again point it at her son. "You brought this on yourself.

Maybe a few years in the Gloom will teach you a lesson."

"Alex!" Kirbie yelled from behind him.

The Umbra Gun fired, aimed at Alex's chest, but he stood tall. Thrusting his arm out, he focused on the black, glimmering ball of energy and pushed against it with his mind. It slowed until it came to a stop right in front his outstretched palm, causing his Cloak mark to surface and his hand to freeze. Then he did the only natural thing—the thing that he had perfected in his training sessions. He took the energy and flung it back where it had come from.

Shade realized what was happening before anyone else and jumped to one side as the black mass sailed back at her. Unfortunately for the others, it was impossible for everyone to dodge successfully. The energy struck Alex's father in the stomach. Volt looked at his wife, his mouth falling open as the darkness washed over him. In a few seconds he was immersed, and his body, like Lone Star's, melted away.

"Shade?" Phantom asked.

"Leave him for now," she said. "We'll get him on the way back."

She handed the gun off to Titan—it was of no use against her son now.

"Very good," she said to Alex. "Even now I can see myself in you. In your rage."

"I am not like you," he said. "I never will be."

Alex's hands fell to his sides, shaking as he focused on the individual members of Cloak, concentrating on the energy crackling around their bodies. Their satisfied expressions were beginning to drop away. Barrage hurled several balls of energy at Alex, but they never came close to hitting him, instead flying away and exploding somewhere on the other side of the room.

Alex had never felt so much raw power. It was as if the very air was under his control, each molecule charged and ready to react to his thoughts. The bits of table and tile and other refuse on the ground were lifting up, floating around him as he raised his outstretched arms. His feet rose off the ground, his body moving slowly into the air, his coat fluttering out at his sides. He thought about Kirbie. And Misty. And Gage. Of how much he cared for all of them, how he couldn't lose them. He had to save them.

His mother's eyes grew wide, sensing his great power. All of them could see it now, his blue energy crackling in the air around them. His eyes blazed like twin blue stars.

"Alexander," Shade whispered, calm, despite knowing what was to come. "It's beautiful."

And with that, Alex flung all the energy forward with one immense push. His former teammates, gathered together, were thrown backward, flying through the debris-filled air or sliding across the ground. They piled up, one on top of the other in a great heap of stunned bodies. Had it not been for the elevators behind them, they would have sailed straight through the floor-to-ceiling-length windows that were shattering around them, sending glass falling from the tower.

The backlash of the blast was unexpected, and Alex found himself sailing through the air as well. He landed with a thud in front of the Junior Rangers of Justice, who were now the *only* Rangers of Justice. Kirbie was by his side immediately. Alex felt weak, but otherwise fine.

"You're okay, you're okay, you're okay," Kirbie chanted over him.

Alex's wild attack had destroyed several pillars in the room, and large patches of ceiling were starting to fall down all around them. Deep within Justice Tower, there was a moaning, as if the walls were crying out in pain.

"I believe your blast has caused structural damage," Gage said, running to Alex's side with Misty in tow. "We must be making our exit."

"Right," Alex said. "Just get the gun and we'll be out of here before they can pick themselves up."

The gathered members of Cloak were struggling to lift themselves from the marble—except for one. Titan was more resilient. He could take a beating and pick himself right back up again. He was on feet already, and in his hand was the Umbra Gun.

"You," he grunted through gritted teeth. Metal shone through parts of his face.

"Titan . . . listen . . . ," Alex muttered. He was frantically pushing energy toward the boy, but it was no use. He was tapped out.

The tower began to tremble above and below them.

"Shut up," Titan said. He held the weapon at his side, the barrel pointing at the ground. "I've been waiting for an excuse to get rid of you for a long time. I guess I should be thanking you for giving me the opportunity."

Misty screamed. Gage stepped in front of her.

"Think about what you're doing," the inventor interjected. "You don't have orders to use that weapon."

"We're better off without you. Without all of you," Titan said. "You can rot in the Gloom together for all I care."

A sound blast from Amp shot past Alex's ear and hit Titan square in the chest, but he was ready for it. The bolt bounced off him and ricocheted back at the group. It smacked Kirbie on the side of her head, stopping her in mid-wolf-transformation and knocking her backward. Slowly Titan began to lift the gun, taking his time, savoring their looks of desperation.

But then Titan's expression changed. He was confused. He tried to step forward, but his legs weren't working. Looking down, he saw frost on his pants, drawing ever closer to his chest. He'd been so caught up in the moment that he hadn't noticed that a hand had slid under the cuff of his pants and grasped his ankle. Mallory was on the ground beside him, her eyes icy and staring up at him in disgust.

"No! No! NO!" Titan screamed, hurrying to aim the Umbra Gun and fire before the freezing took over his body. But he was too late. His arms were frozen now too, and the barrel stopped at a sharp angle, pointing too low for anyone to be in any danger. Within seconds only Titan's head was mobile, and he thrashed it about, shouting, until it too stopped, his face frozen in an expression of pure wrath.

Mallory slowly came to her feet. Behind her, Shade and Phantom were shaking their heads and rubbing their bruised limbs. Mallory looked back at them and over to Alex, her face as measured as ever, but her breathing heavy and anxious. Glancing once more at her Cloak teammates, she started toward Alex and his huddled group of rebels.

"The gun!" Alex called to her.

She pulled on the gun, bracing her foot against Titan's leg. There was a snap, and the gun broke, the light metal casing brittle from the cold. Mallory held the barrel and part of the framing in her hand, the skeletal bomb prototype hanging from it. The Excelsior diamond fell to the floor. Gage was at her side in an instant, inspecting both parts of the weapon.

"We have to get out of here," Gage said. "Immediately."

Across the room, Shade's eyes darted from Titan, to the large chunk of the Umbra Gun stuck in his hand, to

Mallory helping Alex to his feet. He held the other half of the gun now—her two greatest Cloak weapons together at last. She wiped away a trickle of blood that was now streaming from her left temple.

The trembling of the floor became a definite quake. Beams of wood began tumbling from the ceiling. The sky was falling. A few of the remaining pillars shook violently, threatening to crumble at any moment.

"Phantom, open a portal," Shade said. "Get our people back to the base. And pick up my husband on the way."

"What about the rest?" Phantom asked, nodding to Alex and the others.

"I'll worry about them."

Another violent shake, and the ceiling around the stairwell caved in completely. Wood and tile and steel fell on top of the only usable exit from the twelfth floor.

Beside the mangled elevators, Phantom called forth her power and opened a swirling oval of dark energy. She raised her hand and a tendril shot forth, latching onto Titan. It spread over him and the remaining half of the Umbra Gun, until they both dropped away into a black pool on the white marble. Barrage and Julie, both unconscious, were the next to go. Phantom stood at the edge of the portal, waiting for Shade.

"You've put me in quite a predicament, son," Shade said. "You're obviously exhausted. I doubt you could muster enough power to save even yourself right now, much less the others."

Alex didn't want to return to the underground base, but it seemed like their only option. They were far too high to jump, and Kirbie could only carry them one by one. The only way to ensure they all survived was to have Phantom drag them through the Gloom.

"Mother . . . ," Alex said, trying to speak rationally. "If you leave us here, we will die."

Shade stared deeply into his eyes. Her face was oddly blank.

"Do you remember what I said you would become if you decided that Cloak was not for you?" she asked.

Alex kept his mouth shut. He knew full well the word she was looking for. *A liability.*

"That's what you are, Alexander." she said. "I'm sorry, but you won't be coming back with us. Good-bye, my son."

"Mother!" he yelled.

But she didn't care. She turned and nodded to Phantom, who let herself fall into the Gloom. Shade was right behind her, walking into that cold, dark place without reluctance, without turning for a last look at those she was leaving behind. As soon as she was inside, the portal collapsed in on itself and disappeared.

The Cloak Society was gone.

The remaining Betas and Junior Rangers huddled

together near the center of the room. The building continued to shake, each tremble increasing in strength. At any moment, the three stories above them would come tumbling down, burying the young heroes and villains.

Alex attempted to erect a force field around them, but with every falling chunk, the barriers were smashed. Amp and Mallory did their best to knock debris from the air, but they could only hold the rhythm up for so long, before everything caved in on itself. Kirbie tried desperately to turn into her bird form, to whisk some of them away, but she was too frightened to focus and was still injured from the blow to the back of the head and the rebound of Amp's sonic blast.

"What do we do?" Kyle asked frantically.

"Gage," Alex said, "you don't have any brilliant ideas, do you?"

"I am afraid not, my friend," Gage replied. "It seems that this may be the end of us."

Misty was crying. Alex felt helpless—the same sense of powerlessness he'd had earlier in the night, strapped to a chair, watching Kirbie struggle on the other side of the glass.

"Misty," he shouted, rushing over to her. "You have to help us."

"What?" she asked, wiping her face with her sleeve. "What do you mean?"

"You have to use your powers to transport us out of here."

Misty looked terrified, backing away from him.

"I—I can't do that," she said. "I'm not that strong."

"Misty, you can," Alex said. "You did it with Gage at the base and again just a few minutes ago without hardly thinking about it. Here, take my hand."

He reached out and placed his right hand in hers, finding one of Kirbie's with his left. He nodded to Gage and Mallory, and they followed suit. Mallory reached out to Amp, who looked confused, but let his fingers interlace with hers. Kirbie grabbed on to her brother.

"We are *not* going to die here," Alex said to all of them, staring at Misty.

Misty's eyes were brimming with tears. She said nothing, but shook her head ferociously. All around them, the building continued to fall apart.

"Misty," Alex said. "You are our only hope now."

"You can do this," Gage said. "I have faith in you."

"We all do," Mallory said, but her eyes, wide and scared, were on Alex.

Misty took a deep breath and closed her eyes. But nothing happened. The group just stayed there, clutching one another, waiting for the end.

"Come on. Please," Alex said. "You have to try. Misty . . ."

Suddenly Misty opened her eyes. Wide. Determined.

"My name is the Mist," she said as her face started to break apart.

There was a loud crack above them, and Alex looked up to see what looked like the entire thirteenth floor falling down on them. He tried to throw up a shield, but the debris broke straight through. He squeezed Kirbie's hand.

And then, everything went black.

17

STERLING CITY AT
DAWN

Alex gasped, struggling to catch his breath as his eyes fluttered open. The air was damp, thick in his lungs. Tall grass pricked at the back of his neck. Above him, he could see the deep blue of the sky and the last faint glow of stars. Blurry figures were crouched over him, and he fought to make them out as he rubbed his eyes.

"He's awake!" he heard a girl's voice yell to his right. His head was spinning. Finally he could see that the two people huddled beside him were Gage and Kirbie. He sat up, letting his vision drift around the blue world. In the distance he could see a highway, but it looked like it was miles away. Kirbie and Gage were talking to him, their hands patting his back and arms, but he wasn't registering their words. He was trying to figure out where he was, and how he had gotten there.

"Slowly now," he could make out Gage saying. "You've been through a lot."

Then his eyes fell on her, the unmoving girl in a cradle of grass and wildflowers that were too overgrown and intricately woven to have been natural. Misty. Her eyes were closed, her skin whiter than usual. Kyle was bent over her, his nose and cheeks red and eyes puffy.

"No, no, no, no," Alex whispered, stumbling as fast as he could to his feet, half crawling to get to her. "Not Misty. No, please."

"Whoa, hold on," Kirbie said, pulling his right arm over her shoulder to steady him. "It's okay. She's fine. She's just sleeping."

"You're sure?" he asked.

"It's not my specialty," Gage said. "But from my limited medical knowledge, she appears to be suffering from acute exhaustion. I suspect that physically she will be fine once her body recovers from what must have been a tremendous expenditure of energy."

"What do you mean? What happened? Where are we?" Alex asked.

"Look for yourself," Kirbie said, stepping away from him and pointing over his shoulder.

Alex turned to the east. On the horizon, Sterling City sat quiet, awaiting the breaking of dawn. In the dimness of the still-waking morning, he could just make out a brooding cloud rising from near the city's center. Justice Tower had fallen.

"We appear to be situated approximately ten miles northwest of the Sterling City border," Gage said.

"You're kidding me," Alex said quietly. "Misty brought us all the way out here?"

"Yeah," Kirbie said. "She must have kept going and going until she couldn't take it anymore. When we were all put back together, we were here. Both of you were unconscious. Kyle's been looking after Misty."

"Mallory?" Alex asked, looking around.

"She's here too," Kirbie said, pointing to a figure sitting alone, far away from everyone else, half-eclipsed by the tall grass. "It's okay. We're okay."

"We should be safe here for the time being," Gage said. "We're far enough away from base that Phantom should not be able to detect any of you who are marked. But I highly suggest that we seek cover as soon as Misty is able to travel."

"Yeah, of course," Alex said. "Just give me a minute to think and we'll—"

His words were cut short by a body ramming into his own, tackling him from behind. His attacker rolled him over on the ground, landing a punch on the side of his face. It was Amp. Alex could see fury in his eyes, mingling with tears.

"You did this!" Amp yelled. "Look at the skyline. Do you see it? That dust rising over the city. That's everything we believed in turned into a pile of rubble. It's the security of this entire country, all gone because of you."

"Amp," Kirbie yelled, pulling her teammate off Alex and to his feet. "Stop it! What are you doing?"

"He knew," Amp said, shaking off Kirbie's hands. "He knew this was going to happen, and he did nothing to stop it. He got you kidnapped, Kirbie. And now they're gone. Lone Star, Lux, and Photon are gone."

"Amp, listen," she said. "Alex helped us. He . . . he was trying to warn us. If you want to blame someone, blame me. It's my head that they got into. I'm the one who—"

"No, Kirbie," Alex said, wobbling to his feet. "He's right. This was my fault. I should have done more."

"Are we going to stand here and listen to this?" Amp asked Kirbie. "They are *supervillains*. We should take them out now, and then go to the police and start getting all this sorted out."

"And then what?" Alex broke in. "You're going to take on Cloak by yourself? You have no idea what they're capable of. Lone Star was the only one they were afraid of, and look what happened to him."

"STOP IT!" Kyle yelled. He jumped to his feet. "Stop screaming. Stop fighting. I can't listen to this. They're gone. What are we supposed to do? The Rangers are *dead*. They were all we had, and now they're dead."

"That's not entirely accurate," Gage said flatly. "It is true that they're no longer on this plane of existence, but they are not dead. They're simply lost in the Gloom."

"The what?" Kyle asked. His eyes quivered with hope.

"It's a place that exists outside this world," Gage said, trying his best to be precise but comprehensible. "It's the place through which Phantom travels."

"So we can go get them?" Kyle asked, his voice nearing a frenzied tone. "We can bring them back?"

"Traveling into the Gloom is complicated," Gage said. "And finding them within it . . . I would not know how to—"

"Yes," Alex interrupted. "We can bring them back. We'll figure out a way."

He wasn't sure if this was even possible, but he meant every word. If saving the Rangers from that horrible place would atone for what had happened, then that's what he would do.

"Of course," Gage said, surrendering to Alex's gusto. "I'll figure something out."

The five of them stood around in silence for a while. None of them looked at one another, their eyes falling on the underbrush and dirt at their feet. Eventually Kirbie walked toward Misty, stopping to whisper to Alex along the way.

"Go talk to her. She's hardly said a word since we got here."

She nodded toward Mallory, who hadn't moved from the grass. Alex walked over to her slowly. With every step the air around him grew cooler. By the time he stood beside her, he was shivering, thankful for his coat. The dew on the grass was crystallized, the brittle blades snapping as he sat. Mallory stared into the horizon, at Sterling City. Her cheeks were marked with trails of frost falling from each eye.

"Hey," Alex said.

"Hey," Mallory replied.

He let a few moments pass before he spoke again. "Are you okay?"

"Yeah. I'll be fine," she said, wiping the flaking tears away from her cheek. "So that's it then. I guess we don't have a home anymore."

Alex nodded. She was right. They were on their own.

"Thank you for stopping Titan," he said. "You saved us back there."

"You're welcome," she said. "He had it coming anyway."

"Yeah," Alex said. "Yeah, he did."

"We did the right thing, didn't we?" she asked. "Everything you said back there . . . you believe it's true?"

"I think so," Alex said. "I mean, yes. We saved a lot of people. I know that's not what we were raised to do, but it seems like it would fall in the category of being right."

"And what you said about my memory?"

"My mother did something to it," Alex said. "I don't know what, exactly. But I know that she's the reason you don't remember anything."

"And my parents?"

Alex didn't say anything, but nodded. Mallory didn't speak again for a while, processing this information.

"They'll figure out that we survived," she said. "They'll come looking for us."

"We have some time before then. We should be safe for now," Alex said. "Come on, let's go back with everyone else."

A few yards away, Kyle and Gage were on their knees beside Misty, watching her sleep. Amp paced back and forth in a tight line, Kirbie watching from nearby.

"Gage, we broke the Umbra Gun, right?" Alex asked. "The bomb is gone?"

"Thanks to Mallory, it should be irreparable," Gage said. "All they have now is the containment cell—Phantom's stored power. It is possible that they could have another commissioned, but frankly, they would be hard-pressed to find someone who can build one. Even if they did, it would take some time to design another prototype. Months, maybe years."

"We should go to the authorities," Amp said.

"Cloak will be watching the police reports," Gage said. "They're hacked into the entire computer system of the Sterling City government. If any of us go to the police for help, they will know, and they will take us."

"Well, that's just great," Amp said. "So we're stranded out here in the middle of nowhere with nothing but the clothes on our backs."

"Actually, my pockets are stuffed with cash," Alex said, patting his coat. "That's a start."

"That's not all," Gage said, reaching into the pocket of his lab coat. He pulled out a sparkling teardrop—the Excelsior diamond. "I thought this might come in handy."

"Gage," Alex said. "You're a genius! Don't let that thing out of your sight."

"We're all alone," Kyle muttered, his eyes starting to water.

"That's not true," Alex said. "We have each other. And we'll get the Rangers back. In the meantime, someone has to be there when Cloak makes their next move."

"You're asking us to team up with our enemies," Amp said. "With the bad guys."

"Good and bad don't really matter anymore," Alex said. "It's not about being a hero or a villain. It's about protecting each other and the people of Sterling City, who have no idea what's coming. We can do that. We know Cloak. We can stop them when they make their next move."

"Okay," Amp said, after a pause. "Let's give this a try."

"What now?" Mallory asked.

"We wait for Misty to wake up," Alex said. "After that, we head for the highway. We need to get out of Sterling City for a while."

He turned and stared at the city's skyline, his eyes unable to move away from the plume of dirt and dust rising from the north side of Victory Park, where the dome of Justice Tower once stood proudly, glowing.

"Everything is going to be all right," Alex said.

"I believe you," Kirbie said.

The city would just be waking to discover that its guardians were gone. There would be lamenting in the streets, public vigils, anger, confusion. People would panic. But Sterling City wouldn't fall to the Cloak Society. Alex would make sure of that.

The first beams of morning light shot over the distant rooftops. In Alex's eyes, they shone a radiant gold, before the world again faded back to blue.

**THE LINE BETWEEN HERO AND VILLAIN
HAS BEEN BLURRED.**

TURN THE PAGE FOR A SNEAK PEEK AT

THE HOUSE AT SILVER
LAKE

THE CLOAK SOCIETY was written in thick black marker on a sheet of paper pinned to the middle of the wall. Beneath it, on a slightly smaller page, was HIGH COUNCIL. Four index cards were tacked below that, one for each of Cloak's ruling members—Shade, Volt, Barrage, Phantom—with their powers written in Mallory's perfect handwriting. Red yarn stretched out from the High Council leading to other cards and pieces of paper, an adornment that Misty had added one night when dreams of falling ceilings and heroes melting into the shadows kept her awake. To the left, the yarn led to STERLING CITY, which branched out into smaller note cards for government administrators, police officials, and media producers. UNIBANDS, Cloak's non-powered workers living below the Big Sky Drive-In, was another subhead, with a few lists written in Gage's slanting script pinned below. And to the right of the High Council was OMEGAS, Cloak's covert team, the superpowered teens who lived outside the underground base and carried out secret missions only the High Council knew about. The accompanying notes for them were brief. Finally, the path down the center of the wall led to BETA TEAM, now reduced to only two note cards for siblings Titan and Julie, then to GAMMAS, the children of Cloak who hadn't developed powers yet. Alex hadn't had the heart to elaborate on that heading any further.

They hadn't bothered making cards for themselves, the survivors of Justice Tower. Alex, Mallory, Gage, Misty: those who had turned their backs on Cloak, the only world they'd ever known. And Amp, Kyle, and Kirbie: the last of the Rangers not lost in the Gloom.

The wall was in a room they called the Rec Room, but War Room would have been a better name for it now. A map of Sterling City was pinned to the felt top of a pool table and covered in notes and color-coded flags marking important locations like the Big Sky Drive-In, the basement safe house, and possible Cloak targets. The table's cues leaned untouched against the wall beside hand-drawn blueprints of Cloak's headquarters. Still more maps were pinned throughout the wood-paneled room, along with catalogs of the weapons at the High Council's disposal and newspaper clippings from across the country, all looking incredibly out of place among the mounted fish and stuffed ducks beside them on the wall.

The room was on the second floor of a large house located on Silver Lake, a manmade body of water about twenty miles northeast of Victory Park. The small suburb surrounding the lake shared its name, and was a place where people could buy summer homes and vacation without ever technically leaving Sterling City's borders. The house was on the water, with a private beach in a private cove nestled far from prying eyes. It had once belonged to Amp's family, but before he was born—when his father still led the Rangers of Justice—it was turned into a secret retreat for the superheroes. The surrounding properties were bought up and cleared, and the wooded land for acres around was fenced off and marked as a private nature reserve. The house was meant to be a place to regroup if Justice Tower was ever compromised, but it had sat unused for over a decade, all but forgotten.

A "safe house," they all called it, though like "Rec Room," the term wasn't exactly right anymore. None of the seven kids who'd escaped from the collapse of Justice Tower two weeks earlier truly felt safe there, even though the closest buildings were other lake houses located miles away, over the fencing and trees. But then, labels were becoming of less use to them, common words seeming more and more meaningless. They hardly knew what to call *themselves* anymore—hero, or villain, or Ranger, or Beta. They existed in a gray area and felt like strangers in their own world. Like exiles.

Alex sat on a couch, looking at the wall covered in yarn and index cards. Analyzing the wall had become a common practice for all of them, as if by staring at it long enough, they might figure out what they were supposed to be doing. They all hoped that somewhere in the notes and graphs and maps was the key to Cloak's defeat. But so far, that key remained hidden from them.

The morning sun filtered in through a window behind Alex, and he focused on a Polaroid tacked beneath the Beta Team note card. The room seemed to darken a bit as the photograph sparked with blue energy that only he could see. He pulled the pin out and brought the picture forward using his telekinesis, until it hovered in the air a foot in front of him. It was a photo of the Beta Team (or at least, what had *been* the Beta Team before Alex and Mallory became traitors), one of the few items he'd taken with him when he'd left the underground base to meet Kirbie near Victory Park. Right before everything accelerated into disaster. In the photo, he and Julie were grinning. Mallory looked like she'd been caught off guard, her mouth slightly ajar. And Titan smirked, his expression full of self-assurance. Alex studied the picture. The faces staring back at him caused his breath to quicken and dragged up a strange mix of feelings. Shame, anger . . . but also something difficult to place. Something like regret, and a longing to return to the moment the picture was taken, to a time when things seemed much less complicated.

Alex's mind drifted to his mother. He wondered what she might be doing or thinking as he sat in the second-story room. If she was having regrets about leaving her son behind to die as Justice Tower fell apart around him. If she was out there looking for him, even now.

"It's not the best picture." A voice came from behind Alex. "But I get why you can't stop looking at it."

He looked over his shoulder at Mallory, who leaned against the doorway. He offered up a half smile and pushed the photograph back to the wall with his thoughts, reinserting its pin into the worn hole at the top.

"If Amp catches you staring at it like that, he might start up on the whole 'they'll never outgrow their past' thing again," Mallory said. "You should at least think of shutting the door if you're going to get nostalgic."

"I know, I know." Alex sighed. "It's weird. It's not that I miss the underground base, exactly. I mean, there are things I do miss about it, obviously. But . . . I don't know. It just feels like it's been forever since we were there. I never thought I'd want to see the Big Sky Drive-In so badly."

Mallory smiled. She had handled the last few weeks

with her usual poise, even through the arguments, the crying, and the unshakable feeling of helplessness. Alex wasn't sure what he'd have done without her.

"Come on," she said. "Time for a run before the sun gets too high."

Alex nodded. For the first few days after they arrived at the lake house, they'd slept in late and spent most of their time down at the dock, swimming and letting off steam. But they quickly realized that even if they weren't sure what would happen next, the last thing they could do was let their training slide. They needed it now more than ever.

Alex followed Mallory out into the hallway. To his left was the room he shared with Gage, though Gage's twin bed sat empty most nights while he slept on a cot in the detached garage—his makeshift workshop. To the right was Kyle's room. The second bed in there was technically Amp's, but he preferred to spend his time in the house's small, finished attic, a space that his father had apparently used when he wanted to be alone with his thoughts. Alex could sometimes hear Amp pacing above him in the middle of the night.

They made their way downstairs, where there were two more bedrooms: a small guest room where Kirbie slept, and the master, where Misty and Mallory shared an oversized bed.

"Is she still sleeping?" Alex asked, nodding toward Misty and Mallory's room.

"Probably," Mallory said. "She tossed and turned half the night. Bad dreams. But she was completely zonked out when I woke up earlier."

In the living room, Kyle sat in front of the television, his eyes glued to the news. He was much more easily rattled since the fall of Justice Tower. Gone was the fearless Junior Ranger who had once strung Alex up with vines in Victory Park. He'd stopped going by "Thorn" and spent most of his time in front of the TV, jotting things down in a spiral notebook. Kyle told everyone he was watching for clues to help them figure out what Cloak might do next, but Alex suspected he was really waiting for breaking news that Lone Star and Lux and Dr. Photon had miraculously escaped the Gloom, reports that Alex knew would never come. At least, not without their intervention.

"Are they still reporting from Justice Tower?" Alex asked, glancing at the TV. "I thought they made everyone leave so they could finish cleaning up."

"They did," Kyle said. "This is old footage. But you should see the fence they put up around the tower site. Every inch of it's covered with flowers and letters written for the Rangers."

People had flocked to the rubble of Justice Tower

almost immediately after it fell. None could say why they felt compelled to go there, only that they had to see it for themselves. They didn't want to believe what they'd heard. They didn't want to imagine a world without the light of Justice Tower shining as a beacon in the dark night sky.

"There are more of them today," Kyle said to Alex and Mallory. His eyes never left the screen.

"More people?" Alex asked.

"More Powers," Kyle said flatly. "All camped out in the sculpture garden in Victory Park. They're holding some kind of twenty-four-hour vigil."

The Powers were people who had superpowers of their own, though "super" was probably too generous a description for most. They'd begun to show up recently to pay respect to their missing heroes. Some of them wore homemade costumes that related to their code names, or, more often, made them look like second-rate Rangers of Justice. Alex had watched as several of them had demonstrated their gifts on the news— the incredible ability to levitate a few inches off the ground, or the uncanny power to coax a very small flame into a slightly larger one. It was possible that there were real superpowers among them, but mostly they were amateurs, inexperienced and undisciplined. On the TV, a local reporter was interviewing a girl whose long, auburn hair was floating all around her, twisting and braiding with a life of its own.

"What can she do?" Mallory asked.

"Something with her hair," Kyle replied. "She controls it mentally, moving it around and grabbing things."

"Wonderful," Alex said. "Our great hope's big weakness is scissors."

"They're delusional," Mallory said.

"They're dangerous," Amp said, entering from the hallway. "They're untrained and reckless with their powers. If any of them have real talents, they're putting the city at risk. How long will it be before they start showing off to one another and some idiot accidentally sets fire to half the park?"

Amp was only a couple of years older than Alex, but there was a grimness in his voice that made him sound much more grown-up. He'd lost not one, but two sets of parents to the Cloak Society—his mother and father, and his adopted family of Lone Star, Lux, and Dr. Photon—and now found himself on a team with several of its former members. If you could call them a team at all.

"You never know," Alex said. "Maybe they'll end up being helpful."

Amp scowled but didn't respond.

"Where's Kirbie?" Alex asked.

"Outside, waiting for us," Kyle said. "She's fishing again. Or trying to."

Alex peeked out the window. Circling low to the water was a golden bird with an impressive wingspan and an unmistakable uniform. Kirbie. She'd been attempting to catch fish in her talons for several days. She'd had no luck so far, but she kept trying.

"Let's get started," Amp said. Reluctantly, Kyle stood and rubbed his eyes. He left the TV on and followed Amp out the door.

They gathered down at the water's edge. Spotting them, Kirbie landed and took her human form.

"Good morning," Alex said as she approached.

"Hey," she said. She shrugged. "No luck with the fish."

"You shouldn't be wearing the uniform," Alex said. "What if Gage's alarms failed and someone wandered in and saw you?"

"Yeah, well, until he has time to make me something new, I'm stuck in this outfit if I'm taking animal form. It's the only piece of clothing I have that morphs with me, and Gage has more important things to worry about right now than what I'm wearing."

"Are we running?" Mallory asked.

"Of course we are," Alex said. "We have to."

No one challenged his statement. All of them were anxious to do something, anything, that would hinder Cloak. But there wasn't much they could do until Gage found a way into the Gloom. So instead they trained, and went over every detail of Cloak's structure, every facet of its history . . . and they ran.

* * *

When the group returned to the lake house nearly an hour later, they found Misty sitting on the porch, a bowl of cereal in her lap.

"We're almost out of milk," she said, yawning.

"Look who decided to get out of bed," Alex said. He reached out playfully to give her a big, sweaty hug.

"Ew!" Misty said, reeling back. "Don't touch me. You're gross."

"I call shower," Kirbie said as they walked inside.

"No fair, you got all the hot water yesterday," Kyle whined.

"Yeah," she said. "But I was also flying around all morning, trying to catch you dinner."

Kyle groaned and walked back over to the television.

"I think we're almost out of peanut butter and bread, too," Alex said to Misty. "I guess we'll have to go on another supply run tomorrow."

They'd arrived at the lake house with the money Alex had taken from his room in the underground base, then found a stash of emergency cash hidden in a cookie jar. Most of that had gone to Gage to update the security system and start figuring out a way into the Gloom, but they still had plenty of money for the time being. And, if the day ever did come when they found themselves desperate for food, Kyle's ability to control the growth of plants made him a walking produce section.

"Ooh! While you're out, get ice-cream sandwiches, those little frozen tacos you got last time—and does anyone know how to make french fries?" Misty asked.

Alex rolled his eyes.

"Uh, you guys," Kyle muttered. "This might be important. . . ."

On the television, newscasters were cutting in to show some sort of press conference on the steps of city hall. Expecting a statement about the Rangers of Justice, everyone at the lake house quieted. But instead of the mayor, or his press secretary, or the chief of police, someone most of them had never seen stepped up to the podium.

"Oh no," Alex whispered.

"What's wrong?" Kirbie asked. "Who is that?"

The woman at the podium was dressed in a navy suit. Her hair was fiery red, pulled into a tight bun at the back of her head. She wore an expression of deep concern, the corners of her mouth pulled down severely. Text at the bottom of the screen identified her as the head of the Sterling City Council, the governing body second only to the mayor himself.

Alex's eyes darted to Misty, who stood frozen as she watched the television.

"Mom?" she asked, her voice meek and high-pitched.

Alex recognized the woman onscreen from her infrequent visits to the underground base. She was Misty's mother—Phantom's non-powered sister—who served Cloak's interests in Sterling City while the High Council raised her daughter.

All eyes turned to Misty now. The woman began to speak.

"At approximately four p.m. yesterday, a young girl went missing on her way home from school. That girl is my daughter. Her name is Misty, and she's ten years old. I don't know why she was taken, or what her captors hope for in return, but I come to you now, as a community already mourning the loss of our protectors, to beg for the life of my daughter. To beg that she be returned to me safely. I ask that those who took my daughter turn themselves in. I promise you that we will be merciful, that there will be no punishment as long as she is returned. And Misty, if you are watching out there, be strong, sweetheart. Know that your mother is looking for you. Misty, please, come home to me."

"What's she doing?" Mallory asked, rushing to Misty's side and wrapping an arm around her. "Does she really think we'd be dumb enough to give ourselves up?"

"No," Amp said. "But they're making it harder for us to move around in public. Now if anyone sees Misty, our location will get called in to the police."

"Or they'll try to detain us and cause a big scene," Kirbie added.

"This press conference is just for us," Alex said slowly. "To tell us that they know we survived. It was only a matter of time before Phantom realized that she couldn't sense any of our Cloak marks in the rubble. This is their opening move."

On the television, the footage cut to a photo of Misty, taken at the underground base. Her smile spread wide across the screen, the perfect poster child for innocence. A note beneath the photo encouraged any sightings of the girl to be reported to a special hotline.

Misty was silent, but the edges of her body were starting to break apart. Her bowl of cereal shattered against the floor.

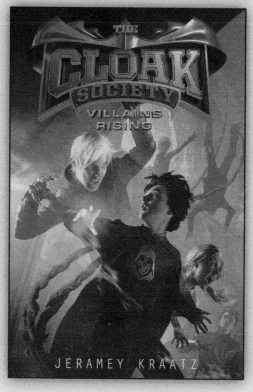